Alex watched his
as he walked through the snow
the camper.

With each step that took him away, her heart felt heavier.

Somehow she'd caught herself before asking him if she could stay for the next few days to help him dismantle his camp. But if he'd wanted her company, he would have let her know.

She was in agony over the knowledge that this would be their last day together. Once he'd deposited her at the Fielding ranch, he'd be off again to take care of sheep business.

And Alex?

She would have to arrange for another rental car to drive back to Jackson Hole airport and fly to New York. To *what* exactly?

The apartment she rented hadn't ever been home to her, only a place to live.

While she fixed breakfast, she looked around the tent. *This* was home to her. In the future, when she thought about Wyatt and the sheep camp in the Wind Rivers, it would always be home in her heart.

Dear Reader,

The inspiration for *Stranded with the Rancher* came from an experience my husband and I had in the high Uinta Mountains of Utah years ago. We were in the Dodge Power Wagon exploring the terrain. For some reason we got high centered on a stump near a band of sheep.

We needed help, but those were the days before cell phones. We figured we'd have to walk out because there wasn't anyone around for miles EXCEPT for a Basque sheepherder. Luckily it was a beautiful summer day. He wandered over to our truck with his dog.

The man was not only friendly and kind, but helpful. He rode his horse over to the ranger station so they could come to help winch us out. We ended up sitting around the sheepherder's campfire. He shared his food and talked about his home in the Basque Country before he'd come to Nevada and then Utah.

After sleeping in the truck all night, we were able to go home, but the experience stayed with me until I found the right book to make my memories come to life. The sheepherder in my book named Pali is my rendition of the wonderful man who came to our aid. I'll always remember him with fondness.

Enjoy!

Rebecca Winters

STRANDED WITH
THE RANCHER

REBECCA WINTERS

H HARLEQUIN® WESTERN ROMANCE

Recycling programs
for this product may
not exist in your area.

ISBN-13: 978-1-335-69971-8

JUN 0 7 2018

Stranded with the Rancher

Printed in U.S.A.

H HARLEQUIN®
TM www.Harlequin.com

Rebecca Winters, whose family of four children has now swelled to include five beautiful grandchildren, lives in Salt Lake City, Utah, in the land of the Rocky Mountains. Living near canyons and high alpine meadows full of wildflowers, she never runs out of places to explore. They, plus her favorite vacation spots in Europe, often end up as backgrounds for her romance novels, because writing is her passion, along with her family and church.

Rebecca loves to hear from readers. If you wish to email her, please visit her website, cleanromances.net.

Books by Rebecca Winters

Harlequin Western Romance

Wind River Cowboys

The Right Cowboy

Sapphire Mountain Cowboys

A Valentine for the Cowboy
Made for the Rancher
Cowboy Doctor
Roping Her Christmas Cowboy

Lone Star Lawmen

The Texas Ranger's Bride
The Texas Ranger's Nanny
The Texas Ranger's Family
Her Texas Ranger Hero

Visit the Author Profile page
at Harlequin.com for more titles.

To all the fearless sheepherders who live through sun, wind, rain, snow, sleet and blizzards in the Rocky Mountains tending the ewes and rams. They make it possible for us to have warm linings in our coats and delicious lamb roasts on our tables. It's an amazing world of beautiful creatures all its own. I was happy to see a little part of it.

Chapter One

Wyatt Fielding exhaled slowly and straightened his back, then knocked on the lawyer's open door. "Mr. Derrick? Your secretary told me to come in."

"Of course, Mr. Fielding. Please sit down."

"Thank you."

"Can I offer you tea, coffee, a soft drink?"

"Nothing, thanks," Wyatt said. Though a cool drink would have been refreshing in the August heat, he wasn't sure he could stomach anything at the moment.

"I'm sorry I couldn't see you until today. I had business out of town all week."

"I understand. When I made inquiries about who was the best attorney in Wyoming, your name came up many times. As I told you on the phone last week, mine isn't truly a criminal case, but what happened to me felt criminal at the time. I left a retainer with your secretary."

The other man nodded. "Go ahead and tell me your story. I'm recording our conversation."

Wyatt cleared his throat, swallowing past the dry

lump there. "Eleven years ago I graduated from high school in Whitebark, Wyoming."

"That's clear across the state."

"Yes. Wind River Country."

"One of my favorite places to vacation. Go on."

"I was in love with a girl and we were expecting a child. We wanted to get married, but she wouldn't turn eighteen until August, so we decided to keep everything quiet until after her birthday, then get married."

"So her parents didn't know?"

He shook his head. "They disapproved of their daughter being involved with anyone. She couldn't go to them. But in July she suffered a miscarriage at six weeks and was taken to the hospital. At that point, her parents would have been told what was wrong. She got word to me at the ranch through one of the nurses. I rushed over to the hospital the next morning to be with her. To my shock, I learned she'd been discharged and sent home.

"I then drove to her house. Her parents told me she no longer lived with them, that I wasn't welcome there anymore, and that I shouldn't try to find their daughter.

"I hurried home to tell my grandparents. I'd brought Jenny to our home lots of times. They knew we were in love and they would have let us be married at home. But under the circumstances, they advised me that her parents were in control. I should wait until I heard from Jenny.

"When a week went by with no phone call or letter, I was half out of my mind and went to the hospital to talk to the doctor who had taken care of her. I was told nothing. I begged the head of the hospital to at least give me some information about her health, about where she'd gone, about the miscarriage. He said he couldn't disclose private records.

"I went back to the ranch feeling as if I'd had an out-of-body experience. That nothing was real. All our plans and dreams destroyed."

The attorney's brows lifted. "To this day you've never had word of her?"

"No. Two months later I went by her house and saw a for-sale sign in the yard. The neighbor across the street said they'd moved with no forwarding address."

"That's a tragic story. I'm very sorry, Mr. Fielding."

Wyatt leaned forward with his hands clasped. "My grandparents raised me after the age of five and have been my mentors. They wanted to get counseling for me, but I fought it. Before my grandmother died, she urged me to talk this out with someone because she knew the experience had changed me. Both she and my grandfather feared I'd go through life carrying this burden."

"Were they right?"

"Yes," Wyatt admitted.

"What brought you to the point you came to me?"

"I'm a sheep rancher and volunteer firefighter. I'm good friends with another firefighter who recently married after being separated nine years from his high school sweetheart. He came back to Whitebark still in love with her memory, and they found their way back to each other."

"Is that what you're hoping? That if you find her, you'll get back together, too?"

Wyatt shook his head. "I don't know. What I'd like to do is find out where she is and how she's doing. I'm praying she's married with children and happy. That would help me a lot. It would probably be too much to ask if she were willing to talk to me about the loss of the baby. Neither of us had closure, but I would never want to disturb her life. Just knowing she's all right would give me peace of mind."

"Are you asking me to find her?"

"Yes. Any information would be helpful."

"All right. Give me the particulars you can about her and her family."

"Her name is Jenny Allen and by now she would be twenty-nine, like me. She was an only child. Her parents were Joseph and Marjorie Allen. I learned they moved to Whitebark, Wyoming, from Hardin, Montana, after she was born.

"Her dad had been a pastor at a church there and took over at the church in Whitebark when the local pastor died. Her father had a widowed aunt in Miles City, Montana, but the woman passed away while we were dating. Jenny might have had family on her mother's side, but I never met anyone. That's all I know."

"Give me her physical description."

"She was five-four, about 118 pounds, slender,

with brown eyes and brown hair she wore swept back in a ponytail. She had a one-inch scar above the elbow of her left arm where she once got cut on the ice as a child. Jenny was soft-spoken."

"Good. Were you on speaking terms with her parents?"

"No. Jenny never invited me to her home. They were very strict, but I had no idea how difficult it must have been for her until the day they closed the door on me. Do you think you can find her?"

"I could, but why not hire a private investigator yourself?"

"I sought you out because I know of the connections you have with people in that field. And I'd just feel better if you handled everything."

"Very well. I've worked with a PI for years. He'll make a search. As soon as I have any information, I'll let you know."

Wyatt got to his feet. "I can't ask for more than that. Thank you very much. I gave your secretary my personal information."

Mr. Derrick stood up and shook his hand. "I hope to have some news for you soon."

Wyatt hoped so, too. His glance fell on a framed maxim hanging on the wall as he said goodbye and left the office.

While we are postponing, life speeds by.
—Seneca 3BC–65AD.

Life *was* speeding by.

During Wyatt's ride to the airport in a taxi, he realized he should have seen about this problem plaguing him long before now. But at least he'd finally done something positive.

Perhaps the attorney wouldn't be able to learn anything, but for the first time since Jenny's parents had closed the door in his face, he had hope. Depending on what he learned, he'd confide in his grandfather, but until he had more information he'd keep this to himself.

An hour later he was winging his way back to Jackson Hole to pick up his car in the short-term parking and drive home to the ranch in Whitebark.

"HEY, MOM, HOW are you?" Alex Dorney was walking around her small Manhattan apartment getting ready to leave on another business trip.

"Well, I'm fine. How lucky to hear from my long-lost daughter!"

"Long-lost is right. I'm sorry, but I was knee-deep finishing up another deadline for the magazine when I was in Florida."

"Since you're back, come on home this weekend. We've missed you."

Her family, including her married brother, Jeff, and his wife, Natalie, lived in Union, New Jersey. Alex's father was the provost at the university there. Her parents' home was only a half-hour drive from Alex's apartment, but it might as well have been ten hours for the amount of time she'd been able to spend with her folks.

"I wish I could, but I'm all packed and leaving from JFK in a couple of hours to do another story."

"Oh, no, honey. You never take a break these days."

"I like work. Mr. Goff is a great boss who gives me the latitude to do stories as I see them."

"I'm glad to hear that, but it's not an answer. When are we going to see you next?"

"I didn't mean to sound flippant."

"I know, but I'm a mother who has the right to worry about you."

Alex knew her parents had been concerned since her broken engagement. But that had been five years ago!

Her mom suffered because there was no man in her daughter's life, but Alex didn't care about that anymore. Not since her fiancé had told her she was too needy and ought to do something with her life besides wait around for him.

Ken Iverson had been six years older than Alex's twenty-two. He was a corporate attorney in a growing local law firm. He'd just gotten back from being out of town and had flung the stinging rebuke at her during a heated moment when she'd asked how soon they should set their wedding date.

His words had burned into her brain. After saying she was going to take his advice, she'd removed the diamond ring he'd given her and gotten out of his car.

Once she was inside her parents' home, she'd backed up against the closed door, vowing never to be accused of that again. He'd followed her from the car, but no amount of pleading on his part could get her to open it or crack the ice around her heart. She was so done it was scary.

"Where are you off to this time?"

"Colorado, then Wyoming."

"Interesting. I've never been to Wyoming."

"Nor I. The boss calls it flyover country."

"Everyone has said that for as long as I can remember. What are you working on? Is it more exciting than my latest project?"

"Indubitably. Your stuff is dull as dust," Alex teased, though it was the truth. Her mother wrote for different software companies who needed her technical expertise to describe their products. She was fabulous at it. "No offense intended, Mom."

Her mother chuckled. "No offense taken."

"When I get there and am settled into some saloon where they rent rooms upstairs, I'll call and run it by you."

"Wouldn't that be funny, if there was such a place these days?"

"Very funny, Mom. I've got quite a bit of digging to do before I begin writing this one, and I don't want to listen to the drunks below living it up after riding into town on their trusty steeds."

"Maybe you should do a magazine spread on the Wild West of today."

Alex laughed. She loved her mom, who had a great sense of humor. "I can promise that *Rockwell Food Business Magazine* won't be putting out an article like that anytime soon."

"With you on board, who knows?"

Another chuckle escaped. As a student, besides garnering many awards, Alex had been given the NYU Business and Economic Reporting scholarship by the New York Financial Writers Association. The merit-based competition had been open to any graduate or undergraduate student in the New York tristate area who'd been interested in business journalism.

In time, she'd been taken on as a featured writer for the prestigious *Rockwell Magazine*. One of her major objectives was to stay ahead of shifting national consumer purchasing patterns and attitudes. Many CEOs looked to their magazine for new trends.

Money had never been her god, but she had to admit it felt good to know she made more than Ken, whom she'd heard through her brother was no longer with the same firm and still a bachelor.

"When will you be back?"

"Let's see." She looked at her Disneyland wall calendar, given to her by her four-year-old niece, Katy, for Christmas. It hung below her framed graduate diploma in journalism from NYU. "Today's Saturday, the third of September. I'll be home in a week. That will be the tenth."

"Perfect. Let us know what time you get in and we'll pick you up at the airport. Plan to come home with us for a few days."

Home sounded good. "I promise."

"Text me once in a while."

"You, too."

"Stay safe."

"Who, me? *Ciao*."

After hanging up, she reached for the suitcase that held her laptop and digital recorder, then left the apartment. New York was experiencing sunny, seventy-five degree September weather. The wrong time to leave, but she had no choice.

Alex walked out to the street and waited until she saw a Yellow Cab with the middle two lights on the roof lit up. She called out, "Taxi!" The driver stopped. Alex made her way through the crowd and opened the back door. "JFK. Delta Airlines terminal."

Part of her trip would involve interviewing sheep ranchers at Wool Growers Association conventions in Montrose, Colorado, and Casper, Wyoming. According to their websites, those organizations existed to preserve and promote the sheep and livestock industries in their states.

They would be good resources to help her start her investigation and obtain interviews. During her initial research, she'd picked up on a surprising trend in the demand for lamb. If it was a fluke, she needed to find out.

On the way to the airport, it hit her that, despite frequently traveling to new places, there was a sameness to her life. It wasn't bad, but it wasn't infusing her with a sense of excitement or fulfillment, either. She let out a deep sigh. Maybe she was asking too much of life.

"CHIEF POWELL? Do you have a minute?"

The head of the fire station in Whitebark, Wyoming, lifted his head. "Sure. Come on in."

Wyatt entered the private office. "I've just gone off duty and wanted to remind you that I'm leaving for the mountains in the morning. I've already told Captain Durrant, so he knows not to schedule me for a week."

The chief smiled. "So you're off with the sheep."

"Yup. It's that time of year to bring the ewes down to the lower elevation."

"Lots of work."

"You don't know the half of it."

"The weather couldn't be better."

"I agree. Here's hoping that at least eighty-five percent of the ewes are pregnant. The trick is not to lose any of them." That included the thirty Hampshire stud rams.

"Take care, Wyatt, and good luck. See you when you get back."

"Thank you, sir."

He left the station in his car and drove to the Fielding Sheep Ranch just a few miles east of Whitebark. After a grueling twelve-hour shift putting out a warehouse fire, he was starving.

Thank heaven for Martha Loveridge, the part-time housekeeper for Wyatt and his disabled grandfather, Royden. Two years ago, his tough old sheep-rancher grandfather had accidentally shot himself in the leg during a hunting trip with friends in the mountains.

Damage to two of the major muscles and a fracture of the left femur had resulted in a limp, even after physical therapy. Today he needed a cane to get around and couldn't do all the activities he'd loved.

The Loveridges lived on the ranch to the south and had been friends of the Fielding family for years. Since the death of Wyatt's grandmother, Martha had come over to help out. She always left enough food for lunch and dinner. He hoped it was a roast and was already salivating.

After this trip to the mountains, Wyatt planned to hire a permanent live-in housekeeper. Though they compensated Martha well, she was getting older and it was time to make the change.

He drove around the rear of the ranch house and parked his car in the garage. Then he backed his truck out so he could load all his gear for tomorrow's journey.

The first thing he did after walking through the mudroom to the kitchen was lift the lid on the Crock-Pot. Mmm. Pot roast and potatoes. His grandfather's beagle, Otis, pretty much on his last legs, came to greet him.

Wyatt scratched his silky head. The dog's movements had alerted his grandfather that someone was in the house. Royden suffered from a certain amount of hearing loss.

"Wyatt?"

He served himself a plate, gave a few pieces to Otis, then walked into the living room where his grandfather was watching old reruns of *Perry Mason* from his favorite easy chair.

"I'm here, Grandad." He sat down on the couch next to him. Otis planted himself at his owner's feet.

"You had a long shift. Was it an arson case?"

"Nope. An electrical problem started a fire in the Olsen Warehouse."

"How much damage?"

"Half the building gone. It could have been worse." Wyatt looked over, knowing what was really on his grandfather's mind. "Grandad? If you want, I'll ask Martha to stay overnight while I'm gone."

His grandfather made an arm motion that said *forget that*. "I'll be fine. The only thing I'm praying for is that the ewes haven't mixed with those from Les Nugent's herd up there."

"That's what we pay Pali for." Pali was their Basque sheepherder who lived in his camper at the seven-thousand-foot level. "Between him and his sheepdog, Gip, they're as good as they come. You know that or you would never have hired him."

"You're right." But his grandfather was never happy these days.

"I know you're upset because you can't go up with me."

"Damn right I am! Who knows how many predators have been ambushing the flock."

"Pali has a sharp eye and will be keeping count."

"Those sheep are vulnerable to every wolf, mountain lion and coyote in The Winds."

The Winds was what the locals called the Wind River Range here in west-central Wyoming. Hard to believe there was a time when Wyatt had hated these mountains, which were famous throughout the West. Had even been afraid of them.

"Anything else you need to tell me before I start loading up my gear?"

"Be sure you keep a few rams up at the ten-thousand-foot level to find the few ewes who failed to secure mates."

"Will do."

"And make sure they're not mixing with the bighorns. We have enough trouble without transmitting bacteria from our domestic sheep to the wild ones."

Wyatt knew it all by heart. He'd been taught by his grandfather, who was known as the expert in this part of the state. After finishing the last of his dinner, he got to his feet. "If that's it for now, I'll get started packing."

He went upstairs to his bedroom to grab a few things, then began the laborious process of loading the truck.

Besides his US Geological Survey maps and cases of food and water, he had a ton of things to load for survival: a gas catalytic heater; tarps; a large tent and several pup tents, in case he needed to use one to nurse a sick ewe; a privy; a couple of sleeping bags; lanterns; matches; knives; medicine; his rifle and shot gun; ammo; binoculars; extra heavy clothing; boots; gloves; blankets; feed for the horses in case Jose brought them; fishing gear; cooking gear and his CB radio to communicate with ham radio operators in case of an emergency.

The next morning he was up at seven thirty to talk to Jose Rosario, the stockman-cum-foreman, who stayed on the ranch in a cabin located behind the ranch house with his wife, Maria.

Since Wyatt's teens they'd lived here year-round and it was where they had raised their family. Lately Jose helped Wyatt's grandfather by answering the business calls that came through and wrote messages for him. Wyatt asked him to be sure to take any calls for him while he was gone—hopefully one from Mr. Derrick. It had been a month. Maybe Jenny couldn't be found...

By eight o'clock he'd put fresh food and water out for Otis. His grandfather was still in bed and had left his radio on all night at full volume. He could be a candidate for an implant. That was something Wyatt planned to talk to him about when he got back.

With everything done he could think of, Wyatt left the ranch. On his way out of town, he stopped at Hilda's for breakfast and saw a couple of his firefighter buddies. They were in their turnout gear looking grubby. The poor guys must have just returned from a fire.

Porter Ewing called out to him. "Where do you think you're going?"

"Up in the mountains on ranch business."

"You lucky dog. On a day like this, I'd give anything to go with you."

"Tell Captain Durrant and hop in the truck."

"Don't I wish. How soon will you be back?"

"In a week."

"Call me. We'll watch some football and get a card

game going with Holden." Holden was the sheriff, and another single guy always up for a game of cards.

"That's a plan."

Their only plan. They lived in a town of just over 1,300 people. Without a woman on the horizon who suited any of them, none of them had much else taking up their spare time except work.

AT THE JACKSON HOLE airport on Thursday, Alex rented a car and headed for Whitebark, an hour and a half away. She would be leaving for New York day after tomorrow, but had a free day ahead of her now. It was only one in the afternoon. In the morning she'd drive back to Jackson Hole and stay at the hotel she'd already booked. They provided limo service to the airport.

After spending time in Colorado gathering information, she'd flown to Casper to attend the Wyoming Wool Growers Association conference. The people there had been helpful. She'd gathered a lot of useful information. One rancher had told her the best sheep person to interview in the Cowboy State was Royden Fielding.

He hadn't been able to attend the conference. However, they had his phone number on file. She could call him.

Alex had done just that and had ended up speaking to his ranch foreman, Jose. When she told him why she was calling he said, "If you wish to talk to Mr. Fielding, it will have to be in person. He's a little hard of hearing and doesn't do well over the phone."

"Oh, I see. Would he be available if I come later today?"

"Of course."

Hmm. That was easy. "I'll need directions to his ranch." The man had accommodated her and they'd hung up. Then she'd booked her ticket to Jackson Hole.

She bought a hamburger in town. While she ate, she made a reservation at the Whitebark Hotel for the night, then headed southwest on Highway 191 beneath a cloudy sky. It had been beautiful weather up to today.

Alex had thought she'd never seen anything as magnificent as the Teton Range of mountains from the air *until* she found herself looking at the Wind River Range ahead of her.

She let out a gasp at the sight of peaks knifing into the rarified atmosphere amidst pockets of snow. According to the brochure she'd picked up, one of them, Gannett Peak, was over 13,000 feet. *This* was the sheep country the man in Casper had been telling her about?

Though she lived in New Jersey, she traveled quite a bit for her job and was stunned by what she was seeing. Whoever called this flyover country had never once come down to earth and put his or her foot on Wyoming soil or smelled such clean air. She inhaled deeply, appreciating the rugged, primitive beauty all around her.

When she reached Whitebark, she followed Jose's directions to the Fielding Sheep Ranch. Alex drove to the front of the two-story ranch house and got out.

To her surprise, an older woman walked out onto the front porch.

"Ms. Dorney?"

"Yes."

"I'm Martha Loveridge, the housekeeper. Jose said to expect you. Come inside. Mr. Fielding is excited for a visitor."

"Well, thank you. I'm thrilled he would allow me an interview."

She picked up her briefcase and followed Martha inside the house to the living room. It had a cozy, warm feeling.

"Please sit down. I'll tell him you're here. He's hard of hearing, so look at him when you speak."

She nodded. Jose had said the same thing.

While she waited, Alex walked around looking at the framed pictures of different couples and children at different ages on horseback. There were rodeo and formally posed pictures, too, propped on the end tables.

She stopped when she came to the eight-by-ten colored photograph on the mantel. An impossibly gorgeous male, probably in his late twenties, was wearing a firefighter's dress uniform. His luxuriant black hair and blue eyes stole her breath.

Who was he?

Chapter Two

While Alex stared at the man in the picture, a little beagle came running in, sniffing at her.

"Oh…look at you." She leaned over to pet him. "How cute."

"Come back here, Otis," a man's voice sounded. She turned around to see who'd spoken. The house-keeper and a man with silver in his dark hair, probably in his seventies, had come into the room. He walked with a limp and used a cane.

"Martha? I thought you said Alex Dorney was out here."

"This *is* Alex." She smiled at Alex. "Meet Roy-den Fielding."

The older man shook his head. "Whoever named you Alex was crazy. With that blond hair and the face of an angel, you're the most beautiful sight ever to walk inside this house."

His over-the-top compliment came as a total surprise. "Thank you, Mr. Fielding. My legal name is Alexis."

"I still don't like giving a man's name to a woman. Where did you say you were from?"

"New Jersey."

"Ah! That explains it. Sit down and make yourself comfortable."

Alex smiled inside. She would love to know what that meant, but decided not to pursue it and did as he asked. The adorable dog lay at his feet.

"Jose told me you wanted to get some information from me. Why in blazes would a woman from New Jersey want to talk to me about sheep?"

She opened her briefcase and pulled out a recent issue of the magazine. Alex handed it to him. "I write for this publication." She explained about wanting to stay ahead of national trends in the food business and what it meant for the economy. "The little research I've done tells me there's a rise in the demand for lamb, which is unusual. I'm out here to find out why."

"It's about time," he muttered.

Again she didn't quite understand his meaning. "Go ahead and scan some of the articles."

"I'll read yours here on seafood consumption." He spent ten minutes perusing it before looking up. "You really know what you're about, don't you? How come neither mutton nor lamb was even mentioned as a protein source?"

"I had to quote the information I was given from a graph quoting comparisons of meat and fish, but I'm puzzled, too. That's one of the reasons why I'm here."

"But I'm the wrong person to help you with the kind of information you need."

"Why is that? The administration at the Wool Growers Association in Casper said you're the person who has all the answers."

He laughed. "They were just pulling your leg."

Disappointment swept through her. Maybe her subject being hard of hearing made it more difficult to do an interview. "Mr. Fielding—"

"The name's Royden." He cut her off. "You want the nitty-gritty of this business? You need to talk to my grandson, Wyatt. That's his picture on the mantel."

Alex hadn't been able to take her eyes off him since she'd entered the room. "But he's in a fire-fighter's dress uniform."

"He's a rancher and sheepman first. Wyatt knows it all. He ought to, since I taught him everything." The man's gray eyes twinkled.

Her spirits were suddenly lifted again, but she did wonder why he didn't want her to interview him. "Would he be willing to talk to me?"

"He would, but he's up in the mountains right now at his camp."

"How soon will he be back?"

"Day after tomorrow."

She shook her head. "That's when I have to return to New York. My flight is already booked."

"I thought you were from New Jersey."

"I am, but my apartment and the magazine office are in Manhattan. Could I phone him?"

"He's beyond cell range. Can't you stay longer?"

"I wish I could."

"For you to come all the way out here for a story does you great credit, young lady."

Alex laughed. She hadn't been called that since she was a little girl.

"Tell you what. I'll ask Jose to drive you up to the pasture right now. You'll have to stay overnight."

"But I'm not equipped."

"Have you ever camped out?"

"A few times at the beach with my family."

He shook his head. "Not the same thing, but don't worry. Wyatt will have everything to accommodate you. Jose will go back for you tomorrow afternoon. That way you can get an interview with Wyatt before you have to fly home. He'll give you some angles you hadn't counted on."

Mr. Fielding had just offered her a solution and she was going to take it, even if it meant roughing it for a night! She would have to call and cancel her hotel reservation.

"If Jose will do that for me, I'd be very grateful to him and you."

"You sit tight while I give him a call. I'll ask Martha to find my wife's sheepskin-lined parka along with her cowboy boots and gloves. You look the same size as my Ida. She passed away two years ago."

"Thank you." She studied him for a minute. "I'm sorry you lost your wife."

"So am I. When I shot myself by accident out hunting it brought on her fatal heart attack."

Alex's eyes closed tightly for a minute while she tried to take in the gravity of those tragedies. Despite the importance of following through on this assignment for the magazine, she had a feeling his life's story would be more amazing than any information she could glean from his grandson about sheep.

BY LATE AFTERNOON the wind had picked up. Wyatt eyed the roiling clouds and noted the drop in temperature. By nightfall a storm would hit. He might have known the great weather couldn't last. Thank heaven he and Pali had brought down the last third of their thousand head of sheep to the seven-thousand-foot area of scrubland. The Fieldings owned some of it and leased additional acres.

Wyatt would keep the sheep at this elevation until mid-November, then take them down to the irrigated fields where the ranch's crops were grown.

Only three ewes had been lost. His grandfather would be ecstatic to hear about that. Tomorrow they'd have to examine each animal and take care of those needing immediate attention.

While Wyatt was straightening up his camp for the impending storm, Gip started barking. A minute later, Wyatt saw Jose's white truck coming up over the ridge. He honked the horn. The noise brought Pali out of his trailer.

Wyatt's heart failed him. Something must have happened to his grandfather, otherwise Jose wouldn't be here. Unable to bear the thought, he headed toward the truck. But as he got closer, he saw that Jose wasn't alone. He'd brought a blonde woman with him, maybe midtwenties. What in the hell?

When the truck stopped, she jumped down from the cab in jeans and a T-shirt. The cold wind that was growing stronger by the second molded the fabric to her beautiful body. She was also wearing his grandmother's cowboy boots and carrying her parka, of all things.

His gaze traveled upward to her oval face with green eyes as lush as the patches of grass growing in the mountain passes. Her hair was cut in a cute, short style that the wind kept rearranging.

Gip ran over to Jose who got out of the truck and lowered a suitcase to the ground.

"I've brought you a visitor. This is Alex Dorney from back East. She came to the ranch to talk to the boss, but he sent her up here to see you. Since this storm is going to hit soon, I need to get back down the mountain. My kids are home for a few days. I'll be back tomorrow to get her." With those words of explanation, he got into the truck.

"Wait a minute!"

But Jose was too quick for him. Within seconds he'd started the engine and taken off.

Wyatt turned to the woman, who cocked her head. "I'm sorry, Mr. Fielding. Your grandfather said there was no service up here to alert you I was coming."

The old man must he losing his mind!

Judging by her accent, this woman was a New Yorker. "He was right. We need to get you out of this wind before the downpour starts." Noticing that Pali had gone to his camper with Gip, Wyatt grabbed her two cases and headed for his three-man tent.

She followed him inside. The roar of the wind tugging on the canvas told him this was no small mountain squall that would pass over in an hour. He knew in his gut they were in for the kind of violent early-fall storm he hadn't seen for at least ten years.

THANK HEAVEN HE'D had the tent custom made with two entrances. The one could be used for emergencies, in case he was forced to cook on his old Coleman stove and needed the ventilation. He hadn't used it this trip because he and Pali cooked in the trailer.

As for the heater, it had a hose connected to a hole in the tent that allowed ventilation to the outside. Because of the warm weather, Wyatt hadn't bothered to set it up. Who would have thought he'd need any of the equipment this trip?

He lit a lantern and turned to her. "While you change into the warmest clothes you've brought, I have things to do, but I'll be back. Make yourself comfortable."

Wyatt reached for his parka and stepped out of the tent, zipping it up before he raced to his truck. He undid the tarp to unload the gear he hadn't anticipated needing because he would have stayed with Pali. Already he could feel rain droplets. The deluge was about to start.

After making several trips to the tent, he'd grabbed everything necessary and retied the tarp. Just as he stepped inside, the heavens opened. When he glanced at his breathtaking visitor, she was sitting on his camp stool wearing his grandmother's parka and Justin cowboy boots.

She looked up at him. "Your grandfather sent these clothes with me since I didn't bring a coat. I didn't think I'd need one with such beautiful weather everywhere."

"The sudden change surprised me, too. That parka will keep you warm."

"I'm sorry for just showing up like this. What can I do to make the situation better?"

He stifled a frustrated laugh and reached for the extra sleeping bag. After unrolling it, he pulled out the pillow tucked inside. Once he'd grabbed a blanket, he threw it and the pillow on the end of the bag.

"If you want to put your suitcase over here next to your sleeping bag, I'll turn on the heater and warm up our dinner. Then we'll talk."

The fierce wind and rain didn't let up. Wyatt had set up a temporary kitchen near the back opening with his food supplies and heated the coffee on his stove. "Sugar?"

"Yes, please."

He dropped in two cubes and handed her a mug. The steam mixed with the flowery fragrance she'd brought inside the tent. She had moved the stool over to the end of the sleeping bag and brushed her hair. It gleamed a shimmering silvery blonde in the light of the lantern hanging from the ceiling of the tent. The wind gusts had grown worse, causing the lantern to swing.

To his dismay, his attention wandered to the pale

yellow crewneck cotton sweater she'd put on beneath the parka. His gaze fell lower to her legs. The cowboy boots managed to accentuate the elegant length of her figure. He estimated she was five foot seven or so.

Still surprised to find himself in a small tent with a beautiful woman in the middle of a terrible storm, he got busy opening containers of biscuits and beef stew. When the meal was ready, he handed her a bowl of food and a spoon. She thanked him, and he sat down cross-legged on his sleeping bag while they ate.

"Do you think this storm is going to last long?"

Wyatt figured she must be terrified out of her wits, but she handled it with amazing calm. "I'm afraid it's going to go on all night."

"You're kidding! But it's only September!"

He got up to serve himself a second helping. "Ten years ago an early-fall storm swept through the Wind River Range unexpectedly. This feels just like it. I'm surprised my granddad sent you up here." However unexpected the impending storm, a seasoned man like his grandfather must've known it was coming. Was the old man losing his touch?

"Your grandfather was anxious I get the chance to speak to you before I go home on Saturday. I'm certain he didn't know."

Wyatt hated to tell her this, but no one was going home on Saturday, or anytime soon. "Jose has worked for my grandfather for years in all kinds of weather. He must not have sensed how bad the coming storm is, or he would have refused to bring you."

"I'm sure the last thing he wanted to do was drive me up here."

Wyatt glanced at her. "He was just doing what my grandfather pays him to do. Would you like more stew or biscuits?"

"No, thank you. The food was delicious."

He had to admit her polite manner warmed him. Wyatt glanced at his watch. Eight thirty. Before she went to bed she would need to go outside to the compost privy he'd set up in the one-man tent. But it was a little early for that. Wyatt got to his feet and put her bowl over by the makeshift kitchen area he'd set up with a little camp table. His custom-made tent had been enlarged on purpose to handle more gear.

"I have to talk to Pali, but I'll be right back."

After rummaging in his duffel bag for his hooded windbreaker, he put it on over his parka and let himself out of the tent, into the raging storm.

Wyatt ran against the powerful wind and stinging rain to Pali's trailer. Gip must have heard him outside and barked, because his friend opened the door so he could get in fast. The two men stared at each other.

"We're in for it this trip, Pali. Remember ten years ago?" Wyatt had been nineteen back then. Pali had been twenty-three.

The other man nodded. "Twenty-four inches of snow. We were stranded with the sheep for days."

"Yup. It's going to happen again."

"Do you want the woman to stay in here? I can room with you."

"Thank you, but I believe she's nervous and probably won't like being alone. I think it will be better if she sleeps in my tent tonight. Tomorrow could be a different story. Do you need anything before I go back to her? Thank God I brought plenty of food and supplies."

"That's good to know, but I'm fine."

"All right. See you in the morning."

He patted Gip's head before facing the elements again. This time, icy shards of sleet attacked him. It was turning fast. There was going to be a storm the likes of which he suspected Alex Dorney had never experienced.

WRAPPED IN THE PARKA, Alex sat on the stool and drank another mug of coffee. It was great coffee, much better than she was used to, and she was comfortable enough because of the heater Wyatt had turned on. But she continued to shiver at the ferocity of the storm raging outside. If she didn't know better, they could be on Mount Everest, which was a silly thing to think since she'd never been on any mountain.

She didn't fear for her life. Royden Fielding's grandson had already proved he was a breed apart from any man she'd ever met or known. She was convinced he could handle any situation and wouldn't let anything happen to her. But home felt an eternity away and she was stuck up here with a total stranger who hadn't asked for her company.

A man who didn't have the right to be so impossibly gorgeous. Being a writer who made her living choosing the right words, Alex kept coming back to that particular adjective because no other synonym, like striking, attractive or handsome, adequately described him. She wondered if he was married. If so, he didn't wear a ring, and his grandfather hadn't mentioned a wife.

When he came back into the tent, removing his windbreaker and parka, she couldn't decide which look she liked better—the firefighter in dress uniform or the hunky mountain man needing a shave. He wore a long-sleeved wool shirt and jeans that molded to his powerful thighs. The combination of disheveled raven-black hair and eyes that glowed blue was too much. Maybe the lack of oxygen really had affected her.

"Ms. Dorney? The privy tent is right around the side of this one. You can hold my windbreaker over your head while I take you out. Shall we go now?"

"Yes. Thank you."

She'd been worrying about that. After she carried the mug over to the little kitchen camp table, he handed her the windbreaker to arrange before he put his parka back on. "The wind is gusting, so just hold on to my arm."

"Oh—" she cried when she stepped out of the tent. The blizzard blew nonstop snow in her face. She might as well have been blind as he led her to the little tent he unzipped. After he handed her a flashlight, she managed to zip up the tent and do her thing. The whistle of the wind sounded so eerie, she was afraid she'd be carried off into the void.

In any other situation, she'd rather go through this alone, but at the moment she was thankful he was right there when she unzipped the flap again. He pulled her against his rock-solid body and zipped the tent closed, then held her around the waist until they reached the entrance to the big tent. The warmth and safety of it *and* him, felt like heaven.

He took the windbreaker and shook off some of the snow before zipping them inside. Alex walked over to the heater and knelt in front of it for a minute.

"More coffee?"

"No, thank you. I think I'd better not."

"Smart girl."

"More like desperate."

When she stood up, she found him smiling. It warmed every ounce of her body. The high altitude couldn't be blamed this time for turning her legs into traitors.

"Here I thought I'd be staying overnight in a saloon with rooms upstairs when I drove into Whitebark."

"And a bunch of rowdy cowhands throwing a week's pay at you for the chance to be up there with you?"

She laughed. "Something like that."

One black brow lifted wickedly. "The place exists."

Her smile faded. "I'd rather be here with you."

Her voice throbbed. "Thank you for helping me. I know I was the last thing on earth you expected to see arrive with the storm."

His hands went to his hips in an unconscious male stance that made him even more desirable. *Utterly desirable.* "You're right about that, but I admire your calm."

"Thank you."

Those piercing blue eyes played over her. "This has been a long day for both of us. Can I get you anything before I turn off the lantern?"

The lines of his rugged features fit the outdoor life that made him so extraordinary. "Maybe some ear plugs," she teased. The roar of the elements was almost deafening.

"That's probably the only thing I didn't bring with me."

"So I've noticed. 'Everything but the kitchen sink' has taken on new meaning."

A chuckle escaped his lips.

Alex took a deep breath. "I'll never be able to thank you enough for putting up with me when you didn't have a choice. No unwanted visitor was ever treated with better care. I'm ready for bed now." Though she couldn't imagine sleeping with the wind threatening to lift the tent off the ground. She'd worry about brushing her teeth tomorrow.

"The heater will go off and on during the night, but you'll stay warm."

This cowboy took care of everything. She removed the parka and laid it over the end of the sleeping bag where she'd spread out the blanket. After sitting on the stool to take off the cowboy boots, she climbed in and curled up on her side while she watched him.

In an economy of movement he tidied the kitchen area. To her surprise he walked over and handed her a bottle of water. "You might get thirsty during the night anyway."

The "anyway" brought more laughter to her lips. His sense of humor shouldn't have come as a surprise, not after meeting his grandfather.

"There should be another word besides thank-you."

His eyes searched hers for a quiet moment before he reached up and turned off the lantern. The moaning of the wind drowned out any noise he made getting ready for bed. It was the loneliest sound in the world. But with him inside the tent, she knew a strange contentment that was foreign to her.

"Ms. Dorney?" came his voice out of the darkness.

"Please, call me Alex."

"All right, Alex. I'm waiting to hear what was so important my grandfather sent a woman fresh from the Big Apple up to sheep country."

"I work for *Rockwell Food Business Magazine*, based in Manhattan as a contributing writer."

"I read it regularly."

She sat up. "You do?"

"It and a dozen other publications that keep abreast of news in the meat industry. Depending on how long you've been writing for them, I might have read one of your articles."

His grandfather's words rang in her head. *Among other things, he's a sheepman and knows it all.*

Alex lay back down, surprised by her own stupidity. Everything was making sense, including the fact that his grandfather read her article thoroughly before asking questions.

"Last Saturday I flew out to Colorado to talk to some sheep ranchers at the Wool Growers Association convention in Montrose. After a few days I flew to Casper to attend a similar convention there. The people in charge told me the best person to ask for information was Royden Fielding."

"Grandad would have liked to be there, but he needed me to take him, and I had to be up here."

If he had attended that convention, Alex would have met both of them there. But it hadn't happened that way. The thought of not meeting Wyatt Fielding bothered her in a way she didn't understand.

"I called and set up an interview this morning, then flew to Jackson Hole."

"And you were spared having to spend a wild night in Whitebark."

She smiled. "Being up here on a mountain with sheep, fighting rain and gale-force winds, is what I'd call the real Wild West. I came to pick your brains about lamb."

He burst into that rich kind of male laughter she loved. "Before I knew you wrote for that particular magazine, I thought you might be a photographer my grandfather sent up so you could get some spectacular photographs of the mountains."

"There's a thought." She clutched the pillow. "So, when do you fight fires?"

"Several times a week when I'm back in town. But I also have a ranch to run."

"Your grandfather wasn't exaggerating about you."

"He always exaggerates," he corrected her.

She could believe it, but she also knew that for Royden the sun rose and set with his grandson. "Before we say good-night, do you mind telling me what you did today before I arrived?"

"Is this for research?"

"Yes." Well, that and she wanted to know everything about him.

"We brought down the last four hundred head of ewes and rams over rough mountain terrain and streams from the ten-thousand-foot level where they've spent the summer. Once we start down, they wander off if you're not chasing them every second. They get lost, caught in shrubs and trees, nearly drown and can fall off cliffs on the way.

"Considering the ewes are pregnant, that makes the journey down more treacherous. If the lamb lovers of this world knew what we go through, they'd pay us billions for the privilege of being served lamb chops and roasts at the dinner table."

"Can I quote you on that?"

"Why not? Now, I don't know about you, Alex, but I'm exhausted. Let's sleep on the subject, and tomorrow I'll answer all your questions after we have breakfast and I check the herd with Pali."

He had to be worse than exhausted. She turned on her other side, away from him, so she wouldn't be tempted to talk anymore. Alex's mind filled with pictures of him chasing *her* instead of sheep all over creation, until oblivion took over.

Chapter Three

Lamb.

Wyatt's tired body shook with silent laughter. He knew where this woman had come from and why. But he didn't understand his grandfather's agenda.

Had he really not known a blizzard of this magnitude was coming? For that matter, Jose had taken off so fast, his swift exit seemed orchestrated.

Wyatt knew his grandparents had worried about him since high school. A month ago he'd told the whole story to his attorney. Was it possible the private investigator he'd hired could find Jenny? Had the miscarriage ruined her life?

How did her parents live with themselves after hiding their daughter where Wyatt couldn't find her? How could they have left Whitebark without telling anyone where they were going? The cruelty of never seeing or hearing from her again had astounded him.

But maybe now he'd be given some information. After eleven years, he prayed to God for some closure on what had happened to Jenny.

His grandparents had hoped and prayed he'd meet

another girl. Of course he'd met a lot of them, but no relationship had touched his heart.

Now, suddenly, a beautiful woman had been deposited at his sheep camp, unprepared and un-equipped, relying totally on him for her survival. If this really was orchestrated by his granddad, Wyatt didn't know the man had such a devious streak. The more he thought about it, though, he didn't buy that this was a mere coincidence.

If this was his grandfather's scheme, then Wyatt couldn't fault the magazine writer who'd played into his grandfather's hands by accident. The innocent woman who slept across the tent from him had been the ideal pawn.

Talk about the perfect storm.

WHEN WYATT WOKE UP the next morning, he pulled on his parka and boots. Alex was still asleep. Look-ing outside the tent, he was reminded of his last thought the night before. This perfect storm had cre-ated a white world! Without the driving wind, quiet reigned, but the snow still fell.

Wyatt stepped outside and whistled. His truck was more than half-buried. He walked with difficulty in the thigh-deep snow. Pali's trailer was barely visi-ble. Imagining that his friend was busy digging out, he went back to the tent for the shovel and started to make a path to the privy tent. Alex would need it when she awakened.

As he came back to the entrance, he almost bumped into her. Their eyes fused.

"Mr. Fielding—good morning."

"It's Wyatt. I think we're long past formalities."

She nodded. "I can't believe all this snow! I never saw anything so beautiful in my life. Maybe this trip will make a photographer out of me. But how do the sheep handle waking up to this wonderland when they can hardly move?"

"Much better than we humans."

"Why is that?"

He kept shoveling as they talked. "Is this the writer asking, or just curiosity?"

"Both."

She had a forthright personality he liked. "Sheep have some very effective ways of keeping warm. Their wool insulates them, holding in body heat and resisting the penetration of water. You'll see snow on their backs. The reason it doesn't melt right away is because the body heat is kept in by the fleece. In addition, they're ruminants."

"What does that mean?"

"They chew on their cuds and have four-chambered stomachs. This process generates a lot of heat. The more forage a ruminant eats, the more heat its body produces.

"Our pregnant ewes, in which growth of the fetus results in heat production, stay even warmer as their pregnancy progresses. In fact, ewes carrying multiple fetuses have to increase their respiratory rate just to get rid of body heat. This is one of the reasons they benefit from shearing during the last six weeks of gestation."

"I had no idea."

"Keeping the sheep outside during the winter benefits both them and me. They need the ventilation and increased exercise. Most of the cases of respiratory disease that I have to treat occur in animals that are housed in a barn during cold weather."

"Why is that?"

"The cause is the buildup of moisture and ammonia in the air. It damages the lining of the respiratory tract, interfering with its resistance to infection. Worse, the stale, humid air transmits viruses and bacteria into the airways. This combination of factors leads to coughing, sinus infections, bronchitis and pneumonia."

"Kind of like children in a day care center."

"Exactly. Sheep that live outdoors breathe fresh, drier air and aren't exposed to fumes. Bronchitis and pneumonia in these animals is rare. That's a plus for me. I have fewer sick sheep and don't have to keep the barn clean."

Happy laughter rippled out of her. She threw her head back to catch some snowflakes on her tongue. The tiny action produced an unexpected spark of desire that flared through him. He didn't like what was happening to him.

"The path to the bathroom has been cleared for you. While you're gone, I'll fix some food. Would you like pancakes, bacon, eggs?"

"All of the above and your delicious coffee. What kind is it?"

"Pali gets it from his Basque relative who runs a coffeehouse in Livingston, Montana. She roasts Arabica beans that are shade grown."

"It's the best! When I return, I'll help you."

After he went back inside, he got busy cooking. Pali would be pleased Alex had shared that compliment. He decided to make enough food for Pali to join them. The less time he spent alone with Alex, the better for his peace of mind.

"Mmm. Something smells good." She'd come back inside.

"Do me a favor and warm this bacon. It's fully cooked already. I'm going to find Pali and ask him to eat with us."

She squinted at him. "You trust me?"

"I don't know. You don't cook?"

"Not if I can help it."

"No matter. Would you rather go get him?"

"Not if you don't want to perform an emergency rescue."

"The trailer is only a few hundred feet away."

"In this snow, it looks a mile. Don't worry. I'll try not to burn it. I did do a little cooking when our family roughed it at the beach."

"What beach was that?"

"The Jersey Shore."

"I'll be right back."

He went outside and started trudging through the snow. As he got halfway there, Pali appeared outside the camper. "Hey, Pali! Come on over to the tent for breakfast."

"Yeah?" A smile broke out on his weatherworn face.

"Yeah. Bring Gip."

"So you got yourself a cook."

He knew where this conversation was headed and cut it off right there. "She's a food magazine writer from New York who wants to know why there's a demand for lamb and where it's headed. My grandfather sent her up here, no doubt thinking it would be a good experience for her to see the sheep in their natural habitat."

Pali shook his head. "That doesn't make sense when he had to know this storm was coming."

Wyatt couldn't have agreed more, but had considered keeping his thoughts to himself. He should've known Pali would pick up on the strangeness of their situation. His grandfather had been up to something to send her up here. "I'll see you in a minute," he called, then trudged through the snow to the tent, stepping in the tracks he'd already made.

Alex looked around when he entered. "Isn't he coming?"

"He'll be here soon." Wyatt walked over to her. "I don't smell smoke."

"Being a firefighter, too, I guess you'd know if there'd been a fire in here."

Yup. But he had news for her. There'd been one set already. It had started last evening when she'd arrived. He'd felt an instant attraction and it had brought a wave of heat more intense than any fire he'd fought with his buddies.

They heard barking. Wyatt undid the zipper and Pali came in, shedding his parka. The dog padded over to Alex who leaned down to pet him. Then she smiled at Pali. "Why don't you sit on the stool to eat?"

"Thank you."

She poured him a mug of coffee and handed it to him. "I was just telling Wyatt how much I love this coffee. He told me you get it from a relative in Montana. Do you think I could order some when I go back to New York?"

That was the second time she'd talked about going home. Why that bothered Wyatt, he didn't want to venture a guess.

"I will make sure of it."

"That's wonderful."

She made plates for Wyatt and Pali, and one for herself. Then she sank down on her sleeping bag and fed a piece of bacon to Gip who looked like he was in heaven as he gobbled it.

"How did you happen to come to the US, Pali?" The writer was at it again.

"I was born on a little farm in Orbaizeta, known for its cheese made from the milk of the Latxa sheep. But there's little money to be made at home, so I left and went to Nevada where I had friends. It was there I discovered there was an opening in Whitebark for a shepherd, so here I am, and I stayed."

"That was my grandfather's lucky day," Wyatt interjected.

"I bet you miss your family."

"Yes. I go back four times a year to visit, but I'm very happy here. You're a good cook."

"Thank you, but all I did was warm the bacon without burning it. Wyatt's the one who deserves the honors."

"I think you do, too, for making the most out of being here in a snowstorm."

"That's nice of you to say."

"I understand you're a food magazine writer."

"Yes. I'm writing a story on the mutton and lamb industry and the reason for the costs. Tell me—do you eat a lot of lamb in your native country?"

"Some lamb stew. But mostly we like blood sausage made from the sheep. We fill them with blood and dry them before adding the rest of the sausage filler."

She made such a funny sound. "For me that would be an acquired taste, I think."

Wyatt chuckled.

"Some things worth relishing start out that way." Pali shot Wyatt a glance with a knowing grin. He'd just sent a message that penetrated the skin and went deep. Wyatt's grandfather had made a big mistake, but there wasn't anything he could do about it right now.

The hell of it was, a part of him didn't want to change a thing.

ALEX SIPPED THE last of her coffee as Pali got up and put his plate and mug on the camp table. "Thank you for the meal. Gip and I are going to take a look around and see if any of the sheep are in trouble."

"I'll go with you." Wyatt followed suit, then the two men put on their parkas and gloves.

"I'll clean up," Alex offered, needing to be practical, considering the situation. Wyatt flashed her a glance from under sooty black lashes. She smiled. "I do know how to do that."

"Terrific. I'm not sure how long we'll be gone, but you have everything here you need."

He was right. Everything and everyone she could ever want or need *was* right here. Who would have thought she would have to fly thousands of miles and end up on a mountain in a blizzard for the ice around her heart to melt? "I'll be fine."

His blue gaze swept over her. "When I get back you can interview me." The men stepped outside, but the dog whined and wouldn't leave.

"Gip!" Pali called to him. "My dog knows a good thing when he sees it. He'll be begging for food from now on."

Alex laughed. "See you later, Gip." The intelligent dog answered with a bark and left the tent.

She stood outside on the path Wyatt had made and watched until they were out of sight. There was still cloud cover, but the snow was slowing down. One look at Wyatt's barely visible truck and she wondered how they would ever leave. Jose had said he'd be up to get her later today, but that wouldn't be possible.

Alex went back inside to do the dishes and straighten the tent. How strange to be doing domestic work like this. Not her normal regimen.

Since the whole area must have awakened to the results of this storm, Wyatt's grandfather would be fully aware of their situation. Being the ultra sheepman, he would know everything had come to a standstill. But probably no one knew how long they would be stranded.

That realization filled her with an excitement she hadn't known in years. Alex would welcome all the extra time given her to get to know Wyatt Fielding better.

Taking advantage of her privacy, she warmed some water. After a quick sponge bath, she brushed her teeth and also gave her hair a good brushing. Then she put on a pair of her designer jeans and a clean blouse. For want of an extra sweater, she wore the same yellow crewneck with it.

Once she found the recorder in her suitcase, she sat down on the stool and talked into it about what she'd learned from Wyatt so far. When he returned, she'd get his voice recording.

While she waited for him, she prepared a list of questions on her laptop. In Casper, she'd made several recordings with experts. Alex listened to them now and planned to discuss what she'd already learned to see if Wyatt was in agreement or not.

When three hours had passed, she put her things aside and went out to the privy. After coming back, she washed her hands, then took stock of the food supplies. Wyatt had stacked canned goods against the rear wall of the tent. The tortillas and ground beef stood out and she decided to make tacos for lunch.

After putting the cleaned skillet back on the little stove, she popped open a can and poured in the beef to heat it. She would use the smaller pan to warm the tortillas. Then she made a fresh pot of coffee.

Before long she heard voices outside the tent and looked toward the opening. She was thrilled to see Wyatt walk inside.

"Sorry you were left so long."

"No problem. I have lunch ready."

"Give me five minutes to set up one of my pup tents outside—we have an injured ewe. Then I'll be back."

Wyatt grabbed the shovel and went back out. A minute later he returned and walked over to a corner where he kept a lot of gear. He carried a tent bag on his shoulder with careless male grace.

She stepped outside to watch him set it up. Then he walked over to the camper. In a minute, he and Pali came from that direction carrying the injured sheep and put it inside. Next, Wyatt returned to the larger tent with the shovel before he reached for a small satchel and went back out. Before long he came in and took off his parka.

"How bad is it?"

"The ewe has a broken leg above the hock."

"Oh, no! Does that happen often?"

"No. It's rare. She must have fallen off a boulder on her way down, but we didn't detect it before the storm hit. Pali makes a great vet." Wyatt washed his hands and dried them with a towel. "He'll tuck the leg up against her body, securing it with bandaging tape. It'll mend in four to six weeks."

"Just like a human."

"Yup. We'll take turns feeding her and keeping the tent dry until she's ready to rejoin the herd."

"The poor thing."

He nodded. "Sheep like to stay together."

"So she doesn't want human company?"

"That depends. They respond by instinct. If you work with them long enough, they'll perceive you as a friend. They are social in the herd, but it's mostly for protection."

"So the ewe won't eat out of my hand."

"She will if she has to, from the hand of the shepherd."

All her preconceived notions about sheep were vanishing in the face of the expert.

"Speaking of food, I've made lunch." Except that it was already three o'clock.

"It smells good. I'll eat first, then Pali can come in while I tend to the ewe."

Alex poured him a mug of coffee. She knew after watching Wyatt to give him three cubes of sugar. He ate and drank standing up. "That tasted good."

Once he'd drained the mug, he shrugged into his parka and put a small amount of packaged food into a metal bowl.

"What is that?"

"It's a feed made up of hay, silage, green chop and crop by-products."

"Do they ever eat fruit?"

"Once in a while, but they get sick on too much. They also like mini pretzels and animal crackers for treats."

On that note, he disappeared. As if the tent had a revolving door, Pali soon arrived.

"Hi! Where's Gip?"

"In the camper. His bark would frighten our injured ewe." He washed his hands and reached for the towel.

"Here are a couple of tacos for you."

His dark eyes gleamed. Pali was probably in his midthirties and a tease. "Wyatt is a lucky man."

She decided to ignore his comment and handed him his coffee. "Here you go."

"Is there a man back home waiting for you?"

"Actually, there are two." Her father and brother.

"That's good. Wyatt needs competition. Too many women fall all over him." That she could believe. "When he's not fighting fires, he comes up here to get away from them."

"Then I don't blame him. It must have angered him to see me get out of Jose's truck."

He shook his dark head. "We're both impressed over how courageous you are to have come up here. I also think the sight of you gave him a heart attack. He's been acting very strange. Except for his grandmother, you're the only woman who has ever stepped foot in camp."

Was he kidding, or did she dare believe him?

"What about *your* girlfriends?"

"Um. I forgot. There've been a few."

She chuckled. "I'm afraid I've invaded your all-male stronghold."

"Don't forget our numerous pregnant ewes." He laughed at his own joke and put the dishes in the kitchen area. "You're such good cook, I'll be back for dinner even if Wyatt wants you to himself." On that note, he left the tent.

Deep down she hoped Pali had spoken the truth.

Alex ate her meal alone before doing the cleanup. Twenty minutes later Wyatt came in. He washed his hands again and then stretched out his amazing male physique on top of his sleeping bag. Turning on his side, he rested his dark head against his hand.

"I'm all yours for a few hours."

Alex swallowed hard at the sight of him lounging there like one of those mountain lions she'd read about, lying in wait for a sheep. "Until your ewe needs you."

"She'll need extra attention since she's going to be a mother soon."

"Do they make good mothers?"

"Yes, but if she were to have twins or triplets, she might abandon one of them, not realizing she could have more than one baby. We have to watch the ewe carefully at the time of lambing."

"What kind of sheep do you raise?"

"Romney Corriedales. They're good for meat and wool. You'll notice their noses are longer."

"The things I'm learning! The last time I ate lamb was the night I went out for lamb shish kebabs. I never once considered what went on in the life of a sheep or a shepherd." Alex sat down on the stool. "Being up here with you has been a total revelation so far."

"Except that you haven't asked me the questions you came to get answers for."

"May I record you?"

He nodded.

Alex reached for her digital recorder. "In doing some background research, I learned that four million sheep were estimated to have lived in Wyoming during World War II, but that amount has fallen to 275,000 in the present day. Why did that happen?"

"After World War II, a generation of American soldiers came home with an aversion to lamb. They'd eaten a lot of rank or corned mutton rations, especially in the Pacific, supplied by New Zealand."

"Corned mutton? Those poor GIs!"

He chuckled. "There were also new polyester fibers replacing wool. Little by little, the sheep numbers declined, and then they plummeted. The old sheep wagons got hauled into barns and sheds or were just abandoned beneath piñon pines or in canyon bottoms."

She shook her head. "I never learned about any of that in school. Come to think of it, I don't remember my family serving lamb often. But it must be coming back. I recently picked up on a surprising trend, an increased demand for lamb at some markets in Manhattan.

"With a little more research I found out the same was true in parts of California and the Midwest. If this is a trend that's going to continue, then what will it do to the economy? I flew out here to do more investigating and want to hear your take on it."

Wyatt was staring at her in an intense way that made her suddenly aware of her own heartbeat. She wondered if he'd even heard her.

"What you've picked up on is true. The demand by US consumers is up, imports are down and prices have soared. We're seeing record prices for lambs, the highest ever by a whole lot. Drought has hurt some producers in Texas, but others in states such as Tennessee, Kentucky, Michigan and Ohio have picked up in sales."

"So that's why your grandfather asked me about mutton and lamb."

"What do you mean?"

"I showed him one of the magazine issues I brought with me. He read the article I wrote on seafood, then asked why mutton and lamb weren't mentioned as protein sources. I explained I'd been given a graph of comparison between meat and fish."

Wyatt nodded. "I can understand why. Last year's May delivery of lamb fetched about $1.39 a pound. This year the price is around $2.20 a pound. Lamb numbers far outstrip those for mutton. Eight years ago about 156 million pounds of lamb was slaughtered at federal- and state-inspected plants, compared with about eleven million pounds of mutton. It angered my grandfather that those statistics weren't mentioned in the article."

"But even so, that's good news for the industry, isn't it?"

"Yes, but here's the dilemma. The price is so high that many small, family-owned restaurants won't carry it. And some meat markets suggest customers eat something else, pay less and enjoy. They refuse to sell it at seven dollars a pound."

"I don't understand that."

He sat up, propped on his elbow, and she had to force herself to not stare at how the movement showed off his impressive arms. "I have a friend in Laramie who owns a meat market and wants to give a quality product for a low price. The other day he said, 'It's impossible with lamb right now to keep a high-quality standard and still offer it at a low price, so rather than charge loyal customers an arm and a leg, I prefer to just say I'm out of it.'

"And yet he says the demand still remains strong. To quote him, 'It's the busiest thing we have in the store and could garner very big sales.' The nontraditional meat markets, including mutton and lamb, but also exotic game meats like boar and venison, have been growing more quickly. It's possible that's partly because it's so hard to get. The vendors and market owners trust their own judgment and are more flexible and serendipitous when making a sale to the right customer—someone who won't be turned away from their business altogether by the high prices. It has surprised everyone, and it hasn't peaked."

"Yet I hear a *but*," Alex interjected.

"Yup. Higher prices have put the meatpackers in a bind. If they raise prices, we run the risk that stores and markets won't buy and sales could plummet."

"What *is* the reason for the escalation in price?"

At this point Wyatt sat up fully, his blue eyes alight in a way that dazzled her. "The increased demand has come amid a drop in supply, in part due to decreased production in Australia and New Zealand, two of the world leaders in production and large exporters to the US."

"I didn't realize how much we imported."

"Australia has about seventy million sheep, down from a hundred and seventy million twenty years ago. The drop has been blamed on the ending of a government support program and extended drought followed by recent flooding. In New Zealand, sheep numbers have dropped from about seventy million to forty million, and many producers have switched to dairy and beef production."

"What about sheep grown here?"

"Some of the giant US superstores want to buy lamb for the next two years to see if it can be sustained. In most places, the demand is up. For how long, no one knows. I can give you a little news tip that isn't well-known yet."

She focused on his rugged jaw, his striking eyes, feeling the tent shrink around them. "What?"

"The sheep association has developed a plan to increase sheep numbers by adding two ewes per operation or by two ewes per hundred. The group also wants producers to increase the average birth rate per ewe to two lambs per year."

"And what would the result be?"

"The program would mean 315,000 more lambs and two million additional pounds of wool for the industry to market."

"There's so much to consider I haven't realized."

He smiled. "Just think about it. This would add $71 million in lamb sales and about $3 million for wool."

"That sounds amazing." She turned off the recorder. "You've told me much more than I came to find out. I can't thank you enough. My boss is going to eat up this story when I've written it. No pun intended." She winked.

Alex planned to write a companion piece on the life of a modern-day shepherd. It probably wouldn't see the light of day. She would keep it for herself. For the rest of the time she was up here, she would take pictures with her phone and the trusty digital camera she took on every assignment. Fortunately he had a generator and she could recharge the batteries.

"You've had your turn to ask questions, now it's mine."

She sensed a change in his mood. "All right."

"It's now my belief that my grandfather sent you up here knowing we'd be stranded. He could have answered all your questions and then some at the ranch house. What's your take on that?"

After putting the recorder back in her suitcase, she looked over at him. "At first, I thought it was because he couldn't hear well that he didn't want to do an interview. I didn't know for sure, but the thought did occur to me after Jose drove away so fast. Your grandfather is quite a character. If this was planned, how soon will I be able to get back to Whitebark?"

"We should be able to drive back down the day after tomorrow or the next. But if we don't show up, I'm presuming Jose will load the horse trailer and drive to the trailhead. From there he'll come up on horseback and bring horses for all of us. Have you ever ridden one?"

"More bad news. At ten years of age I rode a pony around at my cousin's birthday party. If this was your grandfather's innovative idea of Match.com Wyoming/New Jersey, he should have done his research first."

A slow smile broke the corners of his compelling mouth, lighting a fire inside her. "According to Pali, the women can't stay away from you, so I don't understand why your grandfather would think it necessary to go to this kind of trouble."

"He's afraid I'm never going to get married."

The stunning comment caught her off guard. "My parents have the same fear about me. I think it's a parental thing. But since I haven't had that experience yet, I can't speak with any authority."

She expected him to say something pithy in response. Instead, Wyatt got to his feet. "I'm off to start digging out my truck while there's still daylight. When I come back, I'll bring the CB radio. You can play around with it. Maybe you'll get lucky and reach someone who'll be willing to make a phone call home to one of your two boyfriends."

Chapter Four

That Pali!

She had to admit she was delighted Wyatt cared enough to tease her. Maybe he was even a little worried about it. Deep down she hoped that was the case, though she felt a little silly.

With her head lowered, Alex put her hands on her knees. She thought of her mom's last words. *Text me once in a while and stay safe.*

Wouldn't she be shocked to hear from some ham radio operator that her daughter was snowed in on a mountain in the Wind River Range with a sheepherder!

I've never been so safe anywhere with anyone, Mom.

Alex's boss wouldn't be concerned when she didn't return tomorrow. Alex had planned to take some time off to be with her family after this trip and would start another assignment in a week. But right now, her thoughts were on Wyatt.

She pondered the change in him at the end of their conversation. Here she'd thought they'd both been enjoying just talking together when all of a sudden he'd stood up, ending it with an abruptness that had taken her by surprise.

He wouldn't have responded like that unless she'd said something that had disturbed him. Or maybe it was anger at his grandfather for putting them in this predicament.

Oddly enough, after the short time she'd spent with the older man, she found she couldn't dislike him for what he'd done. His funny comments she didn't quite understand had made her laugh. How could you be mad at a man who said you were the prettiest sight ever to darken his doorstep?

In order to pass the time, she lay down on top of her sleeping bag with her laptop. Until the battery died, she'd add comments to bead into the article for when she started her first draft.

Around six she got up to fix dinner, making sure to plug her computer in to recharge. After digging out his truck, Wyatt would be starving. Since Pali had said something about eating dinner together, she decided to get chili and biscuits ready for both of them. As she opened some canned peaches to add to their meal, the two men walked in with Gip, who sniffed around her.

Wyatt carried what looked like an Xbox under his arm and put it on top of her sleeping bag. He hadn't forgotten the radio.

Their glances met. "How's the ewe doing?"

"Probably miserable, but fine."

"Your food's ready."

The men washed up and dinner was served.

"Now for the entertainment." Wyatt turned on the radio. After several attempts he tuned in to a Canadian truck driver named Donald who was taking a load of pipes into Fermont, Quebec. His voice came through crystal clear, amazing her. The three men chatted for a moment about the good weather there before Wyatt's startling blue eyes focused on her.

"We're snowed in on a mountain in the Wind River Range of Wyoming with a beautiful woman who needs to get back to New York. Her boyfriends are going to worry about her when she doesn't fly home on time."

"Now that she's got you guys, what's the rush? Put her on."

"I'm afraid she's busy."

"No I'm not!" Alex leaned down. "Hi, Donald. I never talked to a ham radio operator before."

"Babe—you haven't lived! What are you doing in flyover country?"

She chuckled. "Learning about sheep from some shepherds."

"Sheep?"

"It's a long story. I'm a writer for a magazine."

"You're one of those intellectual types, I bet. Probably went to all the right schools and graduated top of your class from NYU."

"Maybe not at the top, but close."

"What's your name and phone number? I'll look you up the next time I'm in New York. I drive down there every six weeks."

"You don't have a girlfriend?"

"Not at the moment."

In an instant Wyatt took over. "The wind's picking up again, Donald. Your voice is fading. It's been great talking to you." He reached down and turned it off.

"Wyatt—" she cried out.

"What?" He downed another biscuit.

Pali laughed so hard he almost spilled his coffee.

"That wasn't very nice to just hang up on him."

"He'll live."

"I agree that wasn't nice," Pali said and stood up. "You ruined the rest of his night." He smiled at Alex. "Thank you for another delicious meal." His gaze flicked to Wyatt. "How about letting me take the radio for tonight? Maybe I'll find a female truck driver to talk to."

"Be my guest." Wyatt handed it to him.

"Good night, Pali."

"Good night, Alex. Come on, Gip. You can't stay in here with her, even if you'd like to."

"Why did you do that?" she asked after they left the tent.

"Much longer and you would have told him what magazine you wrote for."

"Why did you mention me at all, then?"

By now Wyatt had started the cleanup. "To relieve his boredom and yours."

She walked over to help him. "If you want to know the truth, I've never been so *un*bored in my life."

He searched her eyes. "This wasn't a situation ei-

ther of us could have prepared for. Pali told me earlier he's impressed how well you're handling being
stuck here. That's high praise coming from him.
I give you full honors, too. Not everyone, man or
woman, could have dealt with it as well as you have."

"Thank you."

"So what is the truth about your boyfriends?"

Aha! He wanted to know about them!

Her heart thudded because this was the first real
sign he'd shown that he was interested in her as a
woman. She put the clean pans and dishes aside and
turned to him. "There's been no one serious since
my broken engagement five years ago."

He cocked his dark head. "What about your two
boyfriends Pali mentioned?"

"Oh—you mean my father and brother?"

A subtle smile broke out. "You never bothered to
straighten out his thinking."

She shook her head. "He's too fun to tease."

"What happened with your engagement?"

"You don't really want to know. Excuse me while
I make a trip outside." She walked over to the sleeping bag for the flashlight and left the tent.

Yes. I do want to know.

Damn if it wasn't the fault of Wyatt's grandfather
for engineering this!

Needing to expend some excess energy at this
point, he left the tent to check on the injured ewe and
give her a pain pill. She didn't need more food, but

he replenished the water in the shallow metal bowl. Tomorrow he'd put a fresh blanket down for her.

In another half hour Wyatt had battened down the hatches, brushed his teeth and was ready to turn in. Alex had already crept inside her sleeping bag and was facing away from him.

He turned out the lantern before taking off his boots and parka. On the end of his bag he'd left a clean pair of socks and jeans. Once he'd taken off the pair he'd been wearing all day, he put the other ones on to sleep in and got into the sack.

"Alex?" he spoke into the darkness. "Before we go to sleep, I would like to hear what happened."

"No, you wouldn't. You shouldn't have let Pali take the radio."

"I'd rather talk to you. How old were you?"

"Twenty-two. It was ugly. The true me was revealed."

"You don't know what ugly is until you've heard my story." The residual pain from that experience would always live with him.

"So you're a loser, too?"

She could always make him chuckle. "That's what my friends call me."

"What do they do?"

"We're all ranchers. Porter and Cole fight fires in their spare time. Holden is the sheriff. But let's get back to you. Was the breakup mutual?"

"Ken made a comment that hurt me. In my fury I dropped my engagement ring in the hot coffee he'd put in the drink holder of his car. His fingers got burned trying to retrieve it. I hurried inside the house. He came after me, but I locked the door and told him it was over."

"You really ended it right there?"

"Yes. The comment he made let me know that our marriage would have been a colossal mistake. So I would say yes, it was mutual. But I'm sure he liked blaming it on me so he didn't lose the image of being perfect."

"But you still miss him."

"Not at all. Let's talk about you."

"I was eighteen when my girlfriend's parents moved, taking her with them. That was eleven years ago. I never saw or heard from her again."

After a silence, "Was your breakup mutual?"

He'd known that question was coming. "No."

"Are you still in love with her?"

"The memory of her." But, as he'd told the attorney, he didn't know what he felt. He would need to get back in touch with Jenny and would have to get answers to a lot of questions first.

"It's okay if you don't want to tell me what really happened," Alex murmured. "I'd just as soon no one ever knew what Ken said to me."

Wyatt could relate and rearranged his pillow. "What's your family like?"

"My parents are both eggheads." She told him what they did for a living. "My brother, Jeff, is a dentist and married with a lovely wife, Natalie, and a daughter, Katy. I turned out not to like school that much."

"I thought you went to NYU."

"I even graduated, but I never liked it. Still, it was a means to an end. I did what I had to do."

He smiled. "Why did you feel that way?"

"My friend and I always played house. Our whole ambition was to grow up and get married. No other thinking was involved. That's what a little girl did who played with dolls, right?"

The more she talked, the more he wanted to climb into that sleeping bag with her. "I don't know," he murmured. "I haven't a clue what that would be like."

"How about telling me what it was like to be a little boy growing up in Whitebark."

"I wasn't born here. I grew up in Nebraska with my farmer parents and brother, Ryan, who was a year older. We did chores and played constantly together. One day there was a fierce lightning storm. I was standing on the porch of the farmhouse. A ground current struck all three of them.

"They fell. I ran to them, but two of the workers who helped bring in the hay harvest pulled me away. They took care of me until my grandparents from Wyoming came for me."

"How old were you?" Her voice wavered.

"Five. I don't remember a great deal about the past, but I'll never forget that moment for as long as I live."

"Oh, Wyatt—I can't believe what you had to live through."

"My grandparents did everything to help me, but I became a difficult child. I was one of those people you hear about who have high-mountain phobia. I loved riding horses, but I'd never been around mountains and they terrified me.

"I was sent to counseling, but even with medicine, it couldn't help me rid myself of my condition. Not until my grandfather started taking me camping. We'd come up here in The Winds in small increments at the lower elevations to tend the sheep. He spent hours with me, helping me to overcome my phobia."

Wyatt could tell she was sitting up in her sleeping bag. "Are you still afraid?"

"No. The feeling started to go away by my mid-teens. One desirable outcome was that I learned the sheep business from A to Z. That was a good thing, since I didn't like school."

"That's one thing we have in common," Alex interjected, amusing him.

"At career day, one of the firemen came to talk to any students interested in going to firefighter school in Riverton. That sounded like a school I could handle and it clicked in my brain.

"After my girlfriend disappeared from my life, I told my grandparents about my firefighting idea. They made arrangements for me to go, as long as I combined it with helping them with the sheep. We worked out a system after I graduated from fire school and I joined the volunteer fire department in Whitebark. Several of the guys, like my recently married friend, Cole Hawkins, do part-time, too."

"That explains the photograph of you on the mantel."

"That picture was taken a month ago when Cole

was given the Medal of Valor by the governor. We rode the ladder truck together, so our pictures were taken along with his."

"What did your friend do to receive that commendation?"

"He brought down a family of arsonists single-handedly. Cole's a biologist who works in the mountains, trying to eradicate the brucellosis disease from the elk. A cattle family that lost cows to the disease decided to do some damage and wreak havoc. Cole figured out who they were and they were caught."

"An undercover agent, too. All of you are like renaissance men and can do anything."

"My grandfather would tell you there's a big element still missing from me."

"It's obvious he adores you, with good reason. He got to raise you after raising his own son." Again he heard the tremor in her voice. "Thank you for sharing something so painful and personal. Thank you for being wonderful to me. I'll never forget."

"Thank you for staying so calm after the storm struck. Not everyone could make the most of it the way you have."

"It's an adventure I wouldn't have missed."

"Are you still going to hold out on me?"

"What do you mean?"

"Why didn't things work out with your fiancé?"

"I'm too embarrassed to tell you."

"Maybe when we get to know each other better, you'll break down and tell me."

"It seems to me we're already getting to know

each other really well and I can tell you're keeping something back from me. Otherwise, why did you get up and walk out on me earlier?"

He frowned. "When did I do that?"

"While we were talking about our families being worried over our single status. But that's all right. We each have to live in our own private hell, neither of which is fit for human consumption."

His breath caught. *"Alex—"*

"Hey—don't worry about it. I've lived in mine for five years. You've lived in yours since you were five."

He lay back against the pillow. "You're wrong. My grandparents saved me, and I recovered from the loss of my family a long time ago. But there is one area of my past I still haven't put away."

"Can't you talk about it with your grandfather?"

"I had discussions with both my grandparents, but it never helped."

"Maybe you need more counseling."

"That's what my grandmother said before she died."

"Your grandfather told me she died of a heart problem after he accidentally shot himself."

"She passed away soon after, but it was from pneumonia. He felt so guilty for doing something so stupid when she asked him not to go hunting, he takes the blame for her death and goes on punishing himself. But nothing could be further from the truth."

"Sounds like a real love story."

"They had to be close to take in and raise a troubled child like me."

"In that case, you should take her advice. She sounds like she was a very intelligent woman. I went through a couple of years of counseling myself."

"Did it do any good?"

"Obviously not, or I wouldn't have a problem telling you what happened. Forget my suggestion. Instead, satisfy my curiosity and tell me why you didn't go after your girlfriend, or just get married and ask her to live with you and your grandparents until you two could be on your own. I get the feeling they would have done anything for you."

Wyatt's eyes closed tightly. "You're right about that. But she didn't dare defy her parents."

"Ah. They didn't approve of you?"

"Where do I start?"

"Wyatt—what was the real reason?"

He didn't have to think hard. "Because she fell in love with me. That wasn't part of their plan for her."

"It never is at the age of eighteen, yet I think eighteen is the time when two people experience the purest form of romantic love. Nothing is jaded—anything is possible. All is honest, and desire knows no bounds."

He groaned and sat up. "You're quite the philosopher."

"I'm an idiot. Pay no attention to my ramblings. Look what happened to Romeo and Juliet."

"In a perfect world, you would make a lot of sense."

"But that's not the case and never was. As we're both finding out, there's a lot of life after eighteen, and I wouldn't have missed this experience up here with you and your pregnant ewes for the world. Remind me to thank your grandfather for his machinations when I see him again. It gives me hope to see there's still romance in his soul. Good night, Wyatt."

Good night?

He got to his feet. She was saying good-night now, when she'd just lit him on fire with the words spilling out of that mouth he longed to kiss? "Oh, no, you don't, Alex."

"What?"

Wyatt reached up to turn on the lantern. Those green eyes stared up at him in surprise. She looked too adorable with her silvery-blonde hair attractively mussed. "You really think either of us can sleep now?"

"No," she answered in a quiet tone. "I only said good-night because I was afraid I'd said too much and it had disturbed you."

Tempted almost beyond his endurance to drag her to his sleeping bag, he wheeled around and went over to the kitchen area to make more coffee. That's what he needed. Something—anything—to help him get through this night.

Maybe providence had heard him because he remembered the deck of cards stashed somewhere in his duffel bag. While the water heated, he rummaged through it and found the desired item.

"Do you want coffee?" he called over his shoulder.

"Yes, please."

ALEX WATCHED THE man she felt an attraction for moving around the enclosed space while he made them a drink. Tonight she felt eighteen, experiencing the ecstasy of first love in all its springtime glory. Forget the mountain of snow outside.

It didn't matter if his feelings didn't compare to hers. Maybe they never would. But tonight she sensed he was feeling the growing chemistry between them. He could fight it with all his might, but she felt it when his glances lingered on her.

Wyatt had a secret he refused to divulge. If she was stranded with him long enough, it was possible that in time he wouldn't be able to keep it to himself.

But she would never make the mistake of trying to pry it out of him. She'd learned her lesson with Ken. It had to come from Wyatt, without any help from her, when and if he was ready.

A minute later he put down a blanket beside her sleeping bag. Then he brought them mugs of steaming coffee and sat next to her. To her surprise, he produced a pack of playing cards.

He shot her a piercing glance before shuffling them. "I keep these for an emergency. What's your game?"

The way he was smiling at her, she could hardly breathe. This was going to be fun. "Hearts? I don't know many games."

"Hearts it is. I have my own rules for two players." He proceeded to remove all the threes, fives, sevens, nines, jacks, kings and jokers from the deck, leaving twenty-eight cards. He dealt the first card facedown, then thirteen cards to each of them and the final card facedown.

After about four tries she began to catch on. They played for an hour, laughing and joking. He was so good at it, Alex finally called surrender. Then they started slapjack. She couldn't beat him at anything.

"Where did you learn to play like this?"

"At the fire station while we're waiting for an alarm to go off. Another cup of coffee?"

She shook her head. "No way. Too much caffeine at this altitude is ruining me. I need to go out, then it's time for bed and this time I mean it."

His blue eyes danced. "You think you're going to sleep?"

"I'm going to try."

Ten minutes later she returned to the tent. He turned off the lantern. But no sooner had she climbed under the covers than Wyatt was talking to her again.

"Do you like working for the magazine?"

Her heart raced. She hoped he had a reason for wanting to know. "I work with people I like and get to travel around gathering research. The pay is good. I could never work in an office nine to five. How about you? At this point, would you rather do something else than fight fires in your spare time?"

"I think I'm pretty happy just as I am. You can't beat the camaraderie with the guys."

"And when you want solitude, you've got your

sheep and your grandfather, of course," she supplied. "Sounds like you have the perfect life."

"But he's going to go deaf if he doesn't get some help. The hearing aids do some good, but I'm thinking of taking him to a doctor who does implants."

"They can do amazing things these days."

"It would give him a much better quality of life. He's seventy-six and might still live a long time."

"I certainly hope so. I really liked him. He said the funniest things."

"Then it comes as no surprise he must have liked you, too, sending you up here the way he did."

"Is he in a lot of pain?"

"Not anymore, but he tires more easily."

"I bet he's missing you."

"Like your parents are missing you?"

"Not in the same way. They have each other. With your grandmother gone, your grandfather needs you."

"I need him, too."

His voice had grown husky. It touched her heart. "Do you think he's worried about you?"

"He's been worried about me since the day he took me home with them. But, yes, he's worried right now, though he'd never admit it."

"Maybe he sent me up here to check on you," she teased.

Wyatt let out rich laughter. "No. That's not the reason. Trust me. But I do think that before long he'll send Jose with the horses to investigate."

"What is the plan for tomorrow?"

"Pali and I will spend the day checking on the herd."

She rose up on one elbow. "Will you let me go out there with you?"

"You don't really want to do that and don't have the right clothing."

Please don't shut me out. "I've got your grandmother's boots and her parka. If you'd lend me a pair of your jeans to put over mine, I could roll them up. That would work, wouldn't it? When will I ever get another opportunity to see what you do for a living up close and personal?"

Alex heard a deep sigh come out of him. "Let's see what kind of weather we wake up to in the morning."

Don't push it, Alex.

"Of course. Good night, Wyatt. Is it okay that I said good-night again?"

More chuckling rolled out of him. "There's no danger this time. I think I'm finally tired. It's three in the morning."

"Oh, no—how soon do you have to be out there?"

"At six."

"But you can't! You'll be too tired."

"There's no such word in a shepherd's vocabulary. I'll be back at lunchtime to eat and take care of the ewe."

"What about breakfast?"

"I won't be hungry in three hours. Sleep well."

What she'd give to crawl into his sleeping bag and forget the world. Unfortunately, he needed sleep so he could work in just a few hours. But he'd be back, and she'd be here waiting. It was all she could think about...

Chapter Five

Alex didn't wake up until ten in the morning. Wyatt had disappeared without making a sound. She couldn't believe she'd slept so long.

She dressed in her parka and boots to go outside to the privy. A gasp escaped her lips when she unzipped the entrance and discovered more snow was falling. So far about two inches. Thank goodness she could still see to make her way along the path Wyatt had shoveled for them.

On her way back to the big tent, she glanced at the pup tent and felt a wrench for the poor sheep inside. How lonely for her. Alex walked over and opened the flap, but it was too dark inside to see. "Are you all right?" she asked in a gentle tone.

Baa came a high whine that made her jump.

"So you *are* alive! I'll come back in a minute."

Alex hurried to the tent. She found the box of animal crackers stashed with the other supplies and put a handful of them in her parka pocket. After finding her flashlight, she left for the pup tent. Taking care, she shone the light above the sheep and hunkered down near it, leaving the light on. The ewe had been put on a blanket laid over a layer of hay. It rested on its side with its broken leg taped. The water bowl and empty food bowl were next to her.

"Don't be nervous," Alex said in a low, soothing voice. Her eyes studied every inch of the frightened sheep. She could tell it was anxious the way it tried to raise its head and kept crying *baa*.

All God's creatures had their own kind of beauty. So did this ewe, who had a baby inside her to protect. Alex had no idea if the sheep could even see her clearly. She sat down next to the ewe on the hay.

"I won't hurt you. Here." She took out an animal cracker and put it close to the ewe's mouth.

Alex held it for the longest time. The sheep could smell it, but wasn't tempted. This wasn't working.

"I'm going to stay by you for a while so you won't be alone. I know I wouldn't want to lie here for hours and hours in the dark without anyone else around. Since you don't have a name, I'm going to call you Fluffy. You look like a white fluff ball."

She ate a cracker. "This tastes really good. Wouldn't you like one?" Alex pulled out another cracker and put it in front of the ewe for a few minutes. Nothing. Wyatt had said the sheep would only take them from the shepherd, but she thought eventually Fluffy might come to trust her.

Since she was getting hungry, she ate the cracker and reached for more. "I've never seen a sheep up close like this before, Fluffy. Do you like being up here on this mountain?"

Pretty soon she ate another cracker. "I've never been anywhere like this in my life, but I feel safe. I know you do, too, because Wyatt is taking such good care of you. Did you know he didn't used to like the mountains? I don't suppose you sheep have a fear of them."

There were only two crackers left in her pocket. She pulled them out. "Come on." This time she cupped the crackers in her hand and put them under the ewe's nose and mouth. "I can tell Wyatt doesn't have a fear of anything. But there's something he's keeping to himself. I see sadness in his eyes, too. Since we're stuck up here, I wish he'd tell me what makes him so sad.

"Of course, he doesn't have to tell me anything. He's mad at his grandfather for sending me up here. I don't blame him. I'm useless up here and am an added burden for him. He's got enough troubles worrying about you. In fact, I think he'll be upset with me that I'm in here, so I'm going to leave. But I'll be back later when he's not around, to keep you company. Maybe I'll bring you a canned peach. He said you like fruit."

She was about to get to her feet when the ewe suddenly ate both crackers. It happened so fast she chuckled. "Well, what do you know. Maybe you'll eat some more when I come back later today. Be a good girl. Bye, Fluffy."

WYATT RETURNED TO the tent and discovered Alex's footsteps in the fresh snow. He tracked her to the pup tent, incredulous that she'd gone in there.

After pulling the flap aside and inch, he'd been able to see and hear her talking to the ewe in low quiet tones. The things he'd heard her tell the sheep stunned him so much, he felt Alex crawl inside his heart.

He closed the flap, not knowing if she'd had a pet growing up or if she'd ever been around animals. But he knew she'd never been this close to a sheep before or tried to feed one. Perhaps she was afraid, but she didn't let it hold her back from reaching out to the injured ewe.

In another minute he would announce his presence, but he didn't have to wait that long. Suddenly he heard a high cry from the sheep before Alex emerged from the tent. "Wyatt! I didn't know you were out here."

Their eyes held despite the light snow still coming down. "I just came to find you."

"I was in the tent longer than I meant to be."

"How is the ewe?"

She smiled. "You mean Fluffy?"

He might have known. "Sounds like you two got along well."

"I think she was scared at first. So was I, so I chatted with her for a while. And you know what? A minute ago she ate a couple of animal crackers from my hand."

"Why doesn't that surprise me? Let's go. I'm hungry, but it'll take more than a treat like that to satisfy me. I'm going to fix a big breakfast."

"That sounds good. I slept late and haven't eaten yet, either."

They returned to the tent and removed their parkas. Alex heated the water and washed her hands first. "How are the sheep?"

"So far, so good, but I've got to go out again with Pali to inspect the last of the herd."

"How do you know you're not inspecting the same sheep?"

"They have numbered tags and when we've checked them, we mark it."

"That was a foolish question on my part."

"Not at all. It takes more than a few days to learn everything there is to know about sheep. To be honest, I hadn't thought Fluffy would eat anything from your hand, which shows me how much I still don't know about human and animal behavior."

"She wasn't in a position to do anything about it."

"That's not true. She could have cried nonstop and refused your offering. What amazes me is your willingness to go inside the pup tent at all. I had no idea you were so fearless."

"I was afraid, Wyatt, but I felt sorry for her being out there alone."

He took his turn washing up. "What I want to know is how *you* are."

"I'm fine."

"I admire you for putting up such a good front, Alex, but—"

"But nothing." She came right back. "I'm perfectly comfortable here, though I'm sure you're not happy to be forced to accommodate me. The fact that you and Pali live up here from time to time lets me know I'm safe and will continue to be until I can get back down the mountain."

While she got their coffee ready, Wyatt whipped up pancakes, sausage and eggs. In short order they sat across from each other on their blankets to eat.

"This tastes so good. Isn't Pali going to join us?"

"No." When he'd asked Pali to come with him, his friend had shaken his head. If Wyatt didn't know better, he'd have thought Pali was in cahoots with Wyatt's grandfather. "He'll come for dinner."

"I'll fix it. What time shall I plan for?"

"Expect us by seven."

She poured them another cup of coffee. "Do you think it's going to keep snowing?"

"I'm pretty sure it will stop by evening and that will be the end of it."

"So tomorrow could be sunny?"

He studied her features, especially the way her eyes looked expectant. Naturally she was eager to leave, but a part of him wished they wouldn't be able to break camp for a long time.

"That's hard to say, but the massive storm system has blown itself out. We'll just have to wait and see. Normally there's little snow through here until the end of September."

Wyatt got to his feet to put his dishes over on the camp table.

"Will you mind if I visit Fluffy again?"

He looked back at her. "Tell you what. I'm going to check on her right now. I need to clean out the tent and feed her. She'll also need her meds. After a while, I think she'll be disappointed if you don't show up again. Be sure to take more crackers with you."

"How many?"

"A dozen at most."

"Okay."

Wyatt shrugged on his parka. "Do you need anything before I go?"

"Nothing."

"Liar," he murmured softly before gathering the things he needed, including a small gunnysack of hay in the corner.

By now she was on her feet. "What did you say?"

His head jerked around. "You heard me. You're under my protection. If something is wrong, please don't pretend to be brave in front of me."

She stared at him. "I could say the same thing where you're concerned."

Her comment was unexpected. "What do you mean?"

Alex shook her head. "I'm sorry. I shouldn't have said anything."

He frowned. "I have to get going, but when I get back we'll continue this conversation."

Wyatt unzipped the entrance flap and stepped outside to discover the snow was slowing down. In his gut he knew good weather was ahead, but the knowledge did nothing for his troubled mind.

ALEX LEFT THE tent at five, after working on the first draft of her magazine article. To her surprise it had stopped snowing. That would make it easier for Wyatt and Pali to move around, looking after the herd, but she wouldn't have minded if it had gone on falling. Of course they wouldn't have been stranded forever.

Wyatt had told her Jose would come up with the horses if they were gone much longer. But until then, she would relish this experience with Wyatt as much as possible.

She made her way over to the pup tent and let herself inside, using her flashlight. "Fluffy?"

The ewe let out a couple of high cries.

"Don't be nervous. It's me." She crouched down next to her. "It looks like Wyatt has taken perfect care of you. Everything is so nice and clean. I wanted to visit you and see how you're doing."

She sat down and pulled out a cracker. "You remember me, right?"

This time she only had to wait ten minutes before Fluffy ate the cracker. "Good girl. Have another one." They were making progress. By the time six o'clock rolled around, the ewe had eaten all the crackers.

Alex reached over to pat Fluffy's head and check her yellow ear tag. Number FR410. That had to stand for *Fielding Ranch*.

"I have to go and get dinner ready. But I'll be back tomorrow." As she got up to leave, Fluffy let out a few more high cries. Alex decided it was the ewe's way of saying goodbye. "I'll miss you, too."

She made a detour to the privy tent before returning to the big tent. It felt like home to her at this point. After washing up, she opened cans of spaghetti and meatballs to warm. With peaches and pears for a fruit salad, she thought it made a great meal. Besides coffee, she fixed hot chocolate with the powdered milk and cocoa for dessert.

It was closer to seven thirty when the men came into the tent for dinner. They washed up and let her serve them. They all dug in, eating in comfortable silence. When the dinner dishes were cleared and they were all sipping cocoa, Alex asked, "Are all the sheep accounted for?"

Wyatt shot her a glance over the rim of his mug. "We're missing two ewes and one ram. I'm pretty sure they're still ambling around in the high country. I'll bring my horse up later on and find them. But all things considered, we're in very good shape. How's Fluffy?"

"She ate all the crackers I fed her. I think she knows I'm her friend."

Pali smiled. "She would have made a noisy fuss if she didn't like your company. Once again, I'm impressed. Much longer up here and we'll have turned you into a sheepherder, too."

"Except that I haven't done any work. I've just caused extra trouble for you."

He finished off his hot chocolate and got to his feet. "I'll take your kind of trouble anytime. That meal was delicious, especially the hot chocolate. Thank you for dinner. See you in the morning." He put his dishes on the camp table, then shrugged into his parka.

"Good night, Pali."

"I'll go check on the ewe." Wyatt got up and walked Pali out of the tent with his flashlight.

Taking advantage of the time alone, Alex did the dishes. When Wyatt came back, he would want to get right to bed. After only three hours' sleep last night, he would be exhausted.

While he was with the ewe, she made a trip out to the privy with her own flashlight. After coming back, she even had enough time to brush her teeth and climb into her sleeping bag before Wyatt returned.

"I hope you're not asleep," he said some time later.

Her pulse quickened. "Not yet."

"Is there anything you need before I turn off the lantern?"

"No. I'm fine, thank you."

She heard him get settled in his sleeping bag.

"I have a confession to make. Earlier this afternoon while you were in with Fluffy the first time, I heard you tell her I was keeping something to myself. I should have told you I was standing there by the open flap, but I was afraid it would startle the ewe.

"Since then I've been wondering what your former fiancé said that caused you to break off your engagement. It's going to bother me until I get the answer, so I have a proposition to make. If you'll tell me what was so painful, then I'll unburden myself to you. What do you think about that?"

Alex sat up, surprised he'd overheard anything. She was even more surprised he'd be willing to share something painful with her.

"It seemed that way to me even before you confided in the ewe. The description fits both of us, don't you think?"

Yes. "I guess it does," she admitted in a quiet voice.

"Tell me about your fiancé."

When she thought about him now, she couldn't believe she'd ever been involved with him or called it love. "Ken Iverson was six years older than I was. I met him by accident at Jeff's new office. My brother needed an attorney to help him set up his dental practice.

"He was attractive and asked me out. I'd been attending a junior college and didn't know what I wanted to do with my life. We started dating and fell for each other. In three months we were engaged.

"Soon after that, he went out of town on business. He was gone a week. When he got back, we went out to dinner. After he drove me home, I told him how excited I was and wondered how soon we should set a date for our wedding because our parents would need to start making plans.

"He looked me straight in the eye and told me I was in too big a hurry. We'd get married in time, but right now he had a lot of other things on his mind. Furthermore, he told me I was too needy and should do something with my life, not just wait around for him. A man didn't want a woman who clung to him."

In the next breath Wyatt had hunkered down next to her. "He actually said those things to you?"

She nodded. "That's when I realized he'd jumped the gun on getting engaged and regretted it. I think he might even have been with another woman while he was out of town. His repudiation stung me to the core. But it didn't matter. In that moment I learned what kind of a man he really was."

"What did you say to him, Alex?"

"I told him I was going to take his advice. You know the rest. His words did something to me nothing else could have done. That's when I turned to academics and got into NYU. I was determined never to depend on a man again."

Wyatt had been sitting next to her and put a hand on her upper arm, squeezing it gently. His touch sent a thrill of sensation through her. "I'm sorry you were hurt like that. He never deserved you."

"Thank you for saying that. I agree with you. With me, I think it was a case of falling in love with love, but there was no substance. I've been over it for a long time. Now it's your turn to tell me what hurt you so badly your grandmother wanted you to get counseling."

His hand fell away from her arm. He got to his feet. After pulling the stool close to her, he sat down.

"Jenny and I met in high school and were crazy about each other. I did a lot of bull riding. She came to my events. In the late spring of our senior year we went on some picnics in the mountains after school and ended up making love. We planned to get part-time jobs and go to college together. Eventually we would marry.

"But then she started feeling sick and went to the doctor. Even though I'd taken precautions, she learned she was pregnant."

Alex had to stifle a moan. "Did that thrill you?"

"Yes, and we realized we couldn't put off getting married. I'd turned eighteen in May. Unfortunately, she wouldn't be eighteen until August and we knew her parents wouldn't give their consent for us to be married. Her father was a pastor."

"You're kidding. That had to have complicated everything."

"It turned our world into a nightmare. They were very religious and strict. So we decided not to tell them anything and would wait until her birthday, then we'd go to a justice of the peace. I knew we could live with my grandparents.

"But she lost the baby at six weeks."

"Oh, no—"

"The doctor had to tell her parents she'd suffered a miscarriage. When I went to the hospital to see her, I was informed that she had been discharged.

"I couldn't believe the hospital would let her go that fast. I went to her house, expecting to see her. But her parents told me she didn't live there anymore, and they made it clear I wasn't to contact the family again.

"I had no choice but to leave so I went home to tell my grandparents. Two months later I learned that the Allens had sold their home and moved, leaving no forwarding address."

"They just left and never let you speak to her again?" she cried.

"It was as if they'd never existed."

Alex was aghast. "How terrible. Your girlfriend must have been desperate to see you. Did your grandparents try to help you?"

He nodded. "They were wonderful. Grandad talked with an attorney who said they'd had every right to keep her away after she left the hospital because at the time she was still a minor and legally in their care. By the time she turned eighteen, only a short while later, I had no idea how to find her or even where to begin looking."

"Jenny never tried to get in touch with you?"

"No. I'm sure she was terrified of what they might do."

"So all these years you've had no contact."

"None."

"That means you were never allowed to grieve together over the loss of your baby."

Wyatt stood up once more. "I'm still haunted by the fact that I would have been a father. I don't know how Jenny coped, or what has happened to her over the years. I look back now and blame myself for getting her pregnant. If we'd waited until she was eighteen, we could have been married and then made love."

"You were no different than a lot of young lovers, Wyatt, and you said you took precautions."

"It doesn't matter. I was always a loose cannon my grandparents had to worry about. When I discovered her gone without a trace, I nearly lost my mind. That's when they agreed I could go to school to become a firefighter. They knew I needed to find a way to handle what had happened to me."

"Since that time, have you ever considered trying to find her?"

"In the beginning I wanted to. But my grandmother urged me to talk to a psychiatrist for my own sake before putting out a search for her."

"That sounds like wise advice. What has stopped you?"

"Fear."

"Of what exactly?"

"That I've ruined her life while also screwing up my own."

Alex got out of her sleeping bag, unable to contain the sorrow she was feeling for him. "From my vantage point, you're a man who seems to have lived a remarkable life in a lot of ways."

An angry laugh broke from him. "Grandad would tell you otherwise."

She'd already put two and two together. "So that's why he's afraid you won't ever get married. He knows you blame yourself for what happened and can't get past it. Is he right about that?"

"What do you think?"

"It doesn't matter what I think. But the fact that you've had a hard time opening up means you could use someone objective to talk to." She paused. "It was probably too soon to know the gender of the baby."

"I don't have any information. The hospital record was sealed."

"What a cruel thing was done to you and to her! I'm so sorry. After this long a time, maybe you could hire an someone to look into the situation for you just to give you some closure."

Wyatt put his hands on her shoulders. Their bodies and mouths were only inches apart, making it hard for her to breathe. "I already have. Last month I hired someone in Cheyenne to find her."

"That's wonderful! But I take it you haven't heard back yet."

"No. It may be impossible to find her."

"Oh, I hope not," she said with her heart in her voice.

"You're very sweet to be so concerned. I heard the way you were talking to Fluffy. There's a kindness in you she sensed. Even Gip, who's a one-man dog, wants to hang around you. It's a gift."

"That's because I fed both of them."

"No. It goes much deeper than that."

"I wish there was something I could do for you."

"You already have by listening to me. Besides Pali and my grandparents, it's nice to be able to confide in someone I can trust."

"I feel the same way." Her voice throbbed.

He kissed her lips gently before moving away from her. "Now it's time we both got some sleep."

The old Alex would have given in to the impulse

to really kiss him back. But this wasn't the time, even if she succumbed to the temptation. She wasn't Jenny, the girl he'd loved and lost. The painful memory of her miscarriage and the aftermath was the only thing on his mind tonight.

As for Alex, she'd learned a lesson five years ago and was hopefully wiser.

She went back to her sleeping bag. After climbing inside, she turned away from him and hoped to fall asleep so she wouldn't be tortured by being this close to him.

If he was suffering the same torture being in the same tent with her, she'd discover it in time. She prayed it would happen soon, because she was dying!

Chapter Six

It took all the moral fortitude Wyatt possessed not to pull Alex into his sleeping bag and kiss her into oblivion. She'd been offering him comfort over the loss of his girlfriend and baby. The last thing she would expect was for him to start making love to her.

There was no doubt they were strongly attracted to each other, but they'd built up trust between them over the last few days. To want more from her at this stage could ruin their relationship while they were up here on the mountain.

He also had to remember that she'd be leaving for New York as soon as he was able to drive her back to the ranch. Alex had an important position with her magazine, and in all likelihood he'd never see her again. Becoming intimate would only complicate the situation. The smart thing to do would be to keep his distance from here on out, but he didn't feel like being smart.

When morning came, he sat up and noticed Alex was still asleep. It was seven thirty. Time for him to take care of Fluffy before he started breakfast.

After getting dressed to go outside, he unzipped the flap, and blinding, strong sunlight greeted his vision. It hurt his eyes. No clouds marred the pure blue sky. Except for the record snowfall that had blanketed the region a few nights ago, it was as if there hadn't been a paralyzing blizzard.

Under other circumstances he would have been euphoric to know there'd be no more storms for a while. But with the sun out in full force, he'd have to drive Alex back home as soon as he felt it safe to start down the mountain.

Her family might be worried about her and she'd want to reassure them.

He figured they might be able to leave by the afternoon. Once she saw that the sun was out, she'd be the one to ask if they could leave. He had no doubt of it.

Wishing there hadn't been a change in the weather, Wyatt reached for the supplies he needed and headed for the pup tent. "Sorry I'm not Alex," he said after stepping inside. The ewe sounded her high *baa* cry while he made her comfortable and gave her water with her pill.

When he stepped out a few minutes later, there was Alex, coming toward him in her jeans and parka. Her gleaming blond hair was still enticingly tousled from sleep.

"I saw you leave and brought some more treats for Fluffy." To his surprise, she didn't comment on the change in the weather and didn't look particularly happy.

"I'm sure she'll love them. But since she's just eaten, why don't you save them for later? She'll appreciate them more after Pali and I transfer her to the back of my truck."

"What do you mean?"

"After we make another inspection of the herd, I'm driving you down to the ranch later on today." She had no idea how much it was killing him to say that. "We'll take Fluffy with us. Jose will keep her in the barn and tend her."

The light went out of her lustrous green eyes. If it meant what he thought, then he'd just been given confirmation that these nights with him had caused something significant to go on inside of her, too.

"Even if the sun is out, how can we leave while the snow is still so deep?"

"The wind gusted during the night, blowing the snow to make the track more drivable. It's a beautiful day now and not too deep for the truck. It'll be a lot easier for me to manage it down to the trailhead.

"With no more storms forecast for at least the next twenty-four hours, we should take advantage of the time to get you back to civilization. My grandfather will be relieved to see you survived."

Quiet reigned until she said, "I'm sure he'll be overjoyed to give you a hug, too."

He smiled. "I doubt he'll send Jose up here on horseback now. As for your family, you can tell them all is well and make your plans to fly back to New York." Might as well say it and get it over with.

She stood there motionless. "Where will you be after you drop me off?"

"I'll be coming back up here to close down the camp."

"How long does it take you?"

"A couple of days, maybe longer."

Alex started to say something, then held back.

He'd give anything to know what she'd wanted to express. If she had any idea of his feelings for her… "Come on. Let's fix breakfast."

"I'll do it," she offered. "Why don't you invite Pali?"

"You're sure?"

"I'd like to do my part. Will he be staying up here?"

Wyatt nodded. "For another month in his camper. Then I'll come back up in November and we'll bring the sheep down to the grazing area near the ranch until birthing season. Jose will take over while Pali takes a break and goes home for the Christmas holidays."

"I see." After a hesitation, "Do you have a preference for breakfast?"

"Anything you want to fix, but I know our provisions are disappearing."

"Well, if this is going to be our last breakfast together, then I'll open up the last can of bacon to go with the sausage in celebration of our survival."

"And how about some more of that hot chocolate? Pali loves it."

"What about you?"

Their eyes held. "You know I drank three cups of it last time and moaned when there wasn't any more. That should tell you something." *Don't you realize I'm so crazy about you, I don't know how I'm going to handle it after you're gone?* "Be back in a few minutes."

ALEX WATCHED HIS TALL, rock-hard frame as he walked through the snow toward the camper. With each step that took him away, her heart felt heavier. The glorious sunshine that made the snow sparkle like diamonds was the most unwelcome sight she'd ever beheld.

Somehow she'd caught herself before asking him if she could stay for the next few days to help him dismantle his camp. If he'd wanted her company, he would have let her know.

She was in agony over the knowledge that this would be their last day together. Once he'd deposited her at the Fielding ranch, he'd be off again to take care of sheep business.

And Alex?

She wondered if her rental car had been returned. She might have to arrange for another rental to drive back to the Jackson Hole Airport and fly to New York. To *what* exactly?

The apartment she rented hadn't ever been home to her, only a place to live. She'd left her parents' home a long time ago.

While she fixed breakfast, she looked around the tent where she'd known a completeness with Wyatt that surpassed any other feelings. *This* was home to her. So many memories, created since Jose had driven her up here, were living inside of her. In the future, when she thought about Wyatt and the sheep camp in the Wind Rivers, it would always be home in her heart.

Terrified and depressed at the prospect of having to leave him forever, she hardly noticed what she was doing. By the time the men joined her, she'd made enough pancakes for an army.

They roared with laughter when she suggested they feed the excess to the sheep for a going-away gift.

Pali grinned at her. "Don't worry, Alex. Gip will enjoy them. They'll be his treats over the next few days."

She'd forgotten about the frisky dog who'd been forced to stay in the camper so he wouldn't frighten Fluffy.

Wyatt got up from the blanket and put his dishes on the camp table. "Thank you for another delicious meal. You've spoiled us rotten."

"I'll miss your hot chocolate," Pali chimed in.

"It was the least I could do when you've both taken such good care of me."

Wyatt's brilliant blue eyes flashed her a penetrating glance. "We'll be back by one thirty at the latest to load a few of the things in the truck and get going. The trip up here only took you and Jose an hour and a half, but it'll be quite a bit longer on the way down."

Alex averted her gaze. "I'll have lunch ready when you return."

After they left, she started to straighten the tent and get packed. She had no idea what Wyatt planned to take out to the truck. All she could do was organize. At noon she went out to the pup tent to visit her new friend. By now she was used to the cries made by the ewe.

"Guess what, Fluffy? We're leaving the camp pretty soon. You're going down to the ranch with me. I don't want to go, but I have no choice. Neither do you, so we'll just have to handle it somehow." This time, the ewe ate the animal crackers almost immediately, warming Alex's heart. "The two of us make strange tent fellas, right?"

Once the crackers were gone, she got to her feet with a sigh. "I've got to go and fix one more meal. See you in a little while." Alex patted the ewe's head before leaving the tent and was rewarded with a volley of cries.

She entered the big tent and washed her hands. For lunch they would have more stew and biscuits along with the coffee she loved. The men still hadn't returned by two. While she waited, she reached for her phone and took pictures inside and out, even opening the flap of the pup tent to get a picture of Fluffy. Thank goodness she'd been able to recharge her batteries.

The strength of the sun's rays warmed the air. Alex had the feeling there wouldn't be any more bad weather for a long time. That probably meant that while she was thousands of miles away on another story for the magazine, Wyatt would be up here or down in the town fighting fires. She knew this ache she was feeling for him would only grow worse with time.

When she left the privy tent, she found the men inside the main tent eating lunch. Wyatt followed her with his eyes while she washed her hands. "Thanks for the meal. We're getting started a little late, so I wanted to eat fast."

"What can I do to help?"

"The truck has all the equipment and provisions we'll need going back down. Once you've eaten, you could carry your cases outside. We'll settle Fluffy in the truck and be off."

Alex ate her stew in record time and did the dishes while the men took care of everything else. After putting on the parka, she stuffed some animal crackers into the pockets, then filled Wyatt's thermos with coffee. Ready, she hurried outside with her cases and the thermos, trying not to break down over the pain of leaving.

The men had removed the tarp and had made a bed for the ewe among all the paraphernalia. Alex put her suitcase in the back seat and climbed into the cab of the truck. It was a black four-door Chevrolet Silverado with chocolate-brown seats and looked fairly new. The interior was so warm, she removed the borrowed parka. Her sweater was all she needed for now.

Pali walked over to her side and opened the door.

"Can't let you go without giving you a hug. Here's a sack of coffee I packed for you to take home. I'll put it on the back seat."

It brought tears to her eyes as she reciprocated and kissed his bronzed cheek. "I'll never forget you or Gip. Take care of yourself, Pali. If you ever want to come to New York, you're welcome to stay with me and my family."

He grinned. "You can plan on it."

"Wait—" She pulled out her phone and took some pictures of him. "Now you can shut the door."

Wyatt climbed in behind the wheel. Once he'd removed his parka, their eyes met. If he saw how hers glistened, he didn't comment on it. She put her phone back in her pocket.

"Anything you need or want before we go?"

I don't want to leave! "I'm ready."

"Good. Fasten your seat belt." He turned on the engine. They both waved to Pali, who walked around the back and gave them a push off through the virgin snow. Slowly the truck inched forward until Pali's camper, the tents and the band of sheep disappeared from sight. Soon they were alone in the most glorious mountain scenery she could ever imagine.

Alex had no doubt Wyatt knew exactly where to drive. He could do anything. She peered at his chiseled profile. He needed a shave. With his wavy black hair disheveled, she'd never seen him more breathtaking. He had no idea how much she wanted to beg him to turn around and go back to the greatest happiness she'd ever known. But she knew she wasn't on his mind.

Jenny, the girl he'd loved, the woman who'd carried his child until her miscarriage, had disappeared on him with no explanation. The baby that hadn't had a chance to grow to full term would have been ten years old by now. Those thoughts and more had crippled him emotionally to a great degree. He needed help, something she couldn't give him. She could weep buckets for him.

You're a fool, Alex.

She turned her head away as they made their slow, steady trip down the mountain. It didn't surprise her that he didn't talk and needed total concentration to forge a trail through the snow. But eventually he put on a country music tape that broke the silence. Every so often she saw tracks and he identified the animals for her.

"If you're hungry, there's a plastic bag on the floor of the back seat with some cans of peanuts and trail mix. I keep them there in case of an emergency."

"Something crunchy sounds good." Alex undid the seat belt so she could turn and lean over to get both items. Her body brushed against his shoulder, sending tingling sensations through her system. Then she sat back and fastened the belt again. Knowing he had to be hungry, she opened the cans and they enjoyed the treats.

"I wonder if Fluffy likes the crackers this much."

He gave her a sideways glance. "You mean she hasn't told you yet?"

Alex chuckled. "Maybe those cries were her way of letting me know. I'd like to think my visits perked up her days."

"Is there any doubt?" The way he looked at her made her smile. "Did you have a pet growing up?"

"Yes. We had a bichon called Beauty. Later on we got a pug I called Beastly and it stuck."

Wyatt burst into laughter. "That explains your natural affection and name for Fluffy."

How would she stand it when she could no longer hear the sound of that deep voice she loved?

He made a wide turn that wound through the tall trees he called lodgepole pines. She remembered this area from driving up. It meant they were two-thirds of the way down to the ranch.

As she was gazing at the beauty of the trees, the truck came to a sudden stop. They'd bumped into something beneath the snow. She jerked her head toward him. "What do you think happened?"

"A tree fell during the storm. Stay here." He grabbed the gloves he'd put above the visor and got out of the truck. She watched as he reached down into the snow and smoothed enough away to reveal a trunk. At that point he took his shovel from the truck bed and removed as much snow as possible.

Ten minutes later he got back in the cab. "I'm going to have to use the winch to move it enough for us to pass through. Don't worry. I'll get us out of here."

"I wouldn't believe it if you couldn't."

He darted her a narrow glance. "Your faith in me is surprising."

"Why do you say that? I'm still alive because of you. That says it all. Here." She reached for the thermos at her feet and handed it to him. "Maybe some hot coffee will help after your workout. I put sugar in it already."

Wyatt looked pleased. "I didn't know you'd filled this."

"My sole contribution."

"It's exactly what I need."

She was thrilled she'd done anything that could help him. He poured coffee into the cup and drank until it was gone. Then she took it from him and put the thermos away until he wanted more.

For the next half hour he secured the trunk with the cable. While he worked, she climbed into the rear of the truck to check on Fluffy. The ewe made some cries and ate the crackers Alex fed her. Then Alex climbed back down and took pictures of Wyatt before getting back in the truck.

After he'd finished hitching up the trunk, he got into the truck and backed up before turning on the winch. Slowly the trunk started to move. The painstaking process took time. When it had finally been cleared enough for them to pass through, she let out a deep breath she hadn't realized she'd been holding.

Wyatt jumped out and removed the cable. Again she caught pictures of him putting everything back in place with a dexterity he must have learned riding bulls in the rodeo. That was a sight of a younger

Wyatt she would have loved to see. Surely his grand-parents had taken videos. When they got back to the ranch, she would ask.

"We should be home before dark," he announced once he got back into the truck. Naturally he was anxious to reach the ranch and reassure his grand-father he was all right. But Alex preferred to be stranded with him.

"You're amazing, Wyatt."

"You mean I'm good for something."

"I wouldn't want to be with anyone else. Haven't you figured that out by now?"

He stowed his gloves and started the engine. "That's nice to hear."

Her spirits sank as their drive took them ever closer to their destination. Ever closer to the end of a journey she never wanted to finish. Once they cleared these trees, they'd be able to see the valley below.

Her gaze wandered to Wyatt, devouring the very sight of him. It was then that the truck hit another obstacle. This time Wyatt let out a muffled exple-tive. Who could blame him for feeling frustrated? Another fallen tree lay across their path.

"That storm really did damage."

"You can say that again," he muttered.

Wyatt grabbed his gloves and got out of the cab. It was like déjà vu, except that this time she could tell it was worse.

Alex jumped out and walked through the snow to

him. The sun was going down and already she could feel a drop in the temperature. "What's wrong?"

"Two old trees fell at the same time."

"You're kidding!"

"I can move one of them now. But the other one will have to wait until morning when we have light."

The news filled her with so much excitement, she was afraid he could tell she was jumping out of her skin.

"No problem. While you take care of the first one, I'll climb in the back and fix us dinner. I never had a meal in a truck bed before. Let me do this much while you get busy and make the most of the light."

Without waiting for a response, she put on her parka and went to work. In his stash of food she found chili with pull-off lids and more cans of peaches. They had part of a thermos of coffee and plenty of peanuts and granola.

Alex chatted with Fluffy and fed her some more crackers while she made a space for them to eat. They could sit on a box and a duffel bag. He'd put the lantern someplace. She would use her flashlight until he found it.

Pretty soon he backed up the truck. She could hear the winch. Her watch said seven thirty when he finally approached and climbed inside.

She handed him the flashlight. He had to be exhausted. "How did it go?"

"So far so good."

"I'm glad. If you'll find the lantern, we're ready to eat."

He knew exactly where to look. In seconds light illuminated their whole area of the forest and everything in the truck. His blue gaze traveled over her. "All the comforts of home. Thanks for the meal. How lucky am I?"

Her heart thudded in her chest. She couldn't imagine being in a more romantic setting with Wyatt than right here on his mountain. Her own little piece of heaven. "Except that the food is cold."

"I'm too hungry to care."

"You and me both."

He sat down on the duffel bag and they dug in. She'd poured him another cup of coffee, which he drank straight down. When he'd drained it, he looked at her. "Is there any left for you?"

"I've got this." She lifted her bottled water.

"That's no substitute."

She shook her head. "I'm not the hardworking lumberjack around here. You deserve all the comforts that can be offered."

"I'm sorry I couldn't get you to the ranch tonight."

A burst of honesty caused Alex to eye him without flinching. "*I'm* not, even if you are. If you want to know the truth, I wanted to stay up at the camp and come down with you in a few days. As it is, I'm excited about spending another night in the mountains with you. When will I ever have an experience like this again?"

His black brows were furrowed. He lifted his head to see her better. "Why didn't you say so in the first place?"

"Because you didn't ask me. If I'd questioned you, I might have come off sounding needy."

That compelling mouth of his tightened. "I'm not Ken."

"No," she whispered. "There's no one like you. Jenny knew that. It's why she wanted to be your wife and have your baby." Alex had purposely brought up the other woman's name so he'd be prompted to do something about the guilt he'd carried for so many years. His grandmother had been right about that.

"I'd rather not talk about it tonight."

"I'm sorry. Would you mind if I asked you one more question about her? Then I promise I'll get off the subject."

"What do you want to know?"

"Have you thought that if you found her and discovered she still wasn't married…you two might get together again?" That possibility had been on her mind ever since he'd first told her about Jenny. It tore her apart, but it had to be said.

WYATT EYED HER DIRECTLY. "Over the first year of separation I asked myself that question every day. But too many years have passed since then." *And I've met you, Alex Dorney.* "We're different people now, living different lives."

Since hiring Mr. Derrick, Wyatt had had concerns about how to handle things if the attorney actually found her.

Alex started cleaning up. "Forgive me for bringing her into the conversation. It's none of my business."

"That isn't strictly true. We've confided in each other. As you know, I retained an attorney to find her. The plaque in his office said, 'While we are postponing, life speeds by.' It prompted me to get going on the answers that will help me erase the question marks. If I still don't feel better, I'll consult a psychiatrist to sort through my angst."

"Now *I* feel guilty," she murmured.

"You don't know the meaning of the word. Even if I'd had the money, I couldn't have gone after her and abandoned my grandparents who needed my help. Who even knows where I would've started the search—it could've taken me anywhere and for who knows how long. I was still a kid, and my grandparents reasoned with me that I would only cause her more grief. In time, their advice got through to me."

She shook her head. "But you really did have to live through a terrible experience, Wyatt. My heart goes out to you. Since you've taken steps to find her at last, I hope that any news you hear will be good and bring you peace."

"I do, too. Thank you, Alex." He finished off the last can of peaches. "Now, it's getting cold. Why don't you go back to the cab? I'll settle the ewe for the night before joining you."

Alex patted the sheep's head. "Good night, Fluffy. Remember, we'll be right here." She fed the ewe some more crackers. Her tenderness tugged on Wyatt's emotions.

Before he could help her, Alex put the flashlight and water bottle in her pockets, then climbed over the side and lowered herself into the snow. While she made her way to the cab, Wyatt got busy taking care of the ewe and gave her a pill.

He looked around and grabbed a couple of cans of Vienna sausages and a pack of dried apricots for their breakfast. After stuffing his pockets with extra water, he reached for two thermal blankets and pillows from the duffel bag. Finally, he grabbed the lantern and climbed over the tailgate.

Alex was waiting for him. This would be their last night alone, a reprieve he hadn't expected. Adrenaline surged through his body. He turned off the lantern to soak in the atmosphere. It was one of those magical nights full of stars and the light of a half-moon shining through the trees onto the snow.

Wyatt put the lantern on top of the cab for easy access. Then he opened the rear door and put everything he was carrying on the seat and shut the door. Lastly, he opened the front door on the driver's side. The map light revealed Alex's beautiful features and the sheen of her hair.

The image of her was implanted in his mind and heart. By some miracle, the blizzard had blown this fantastic woman into his life. As far as he was concerned, she was his. And he longed to hold on to her, to keep her here forever...but he knew he had to let her go.

Chapter Seven

"Hi. Did you think I'd never come?" he asked from the open driver's side door.

"Not at all." Alex smiled. "Fluffy needed attention."

"So do you. I want to get you comfortable. If you'll reach around on your right side, you'll feel the lever that will put your seat all the way back. Try it. Otherwise I'll come around and help."

It took Alex a few attempts before she got it to recline. "Ooh, that's great!"

"It's not as flat as a bed, but it'll do for tonight. Now I'll hand you a pillow and blanket."

She took the items and arranged them while Wyatt climbed inside to turn on the heat and her seat warmer. After he'd locked the doors, he reached for his own pillow and blanket, then adjusted his seat to go halfway back. To his frustration, the console kept their bodies from touching.

"Do you want me to turn on some music?"

"Not unless you want it."

"No. I'd rather talk to you. What's your next assignment after you get back to New York?"

He heard a sigh escape. She'd turned so she was facing him. "That's up to my boss. First I have to submit my current article. Then I have a week coming to be with my family before I start another project."

"Will they still give you a week after being detained here because of the storm?"

"I think so."

"If you need proof that it was unavoidable, I'd be happy to supply it."

"That's very kind of you, but it won't be necessary."

His eyes played over her. "Are you getting warm?"

"I'm perfect."

She looked perfect. "I'll have to turn everything off in a few minutes to save the battery. Hopefully you'll be able to fall asleep until morning. But if you should wake up during the night because you're too cold, let me know and I'll turn on the heater again."

"You're too good to be true."

"That's what Pali said about you."

She rose up on one arm. "And what do *you* say?"

Wyatt's breath caught. "I'm going to miss you and your help with Fluffy."

"My help? I didn't do anything."

"Oh, yes, you did. I would have had to stop occasionally to check on her. But you followed your instincts and kept her company, which was what she needed, and gave me extra time to do my job."

"You're not just saying that?"

"Alex—you've been a real asset. Pali and I needed the meals you made. Once the blizzard blew through, I don't think you have any idea what a luxury it was to know we didn't have to prepare our food. Inspecting the sheep under these difficult conditions has been exhausting work. You made it such a pleasant experience, Pali's going to be in mourning for a while."

"He won't be the only one."

A nuance in her voice brought his head around. "What do you mean?"

"I've loved being stranded up here with you, Wyatt. You've treated me like a queen and introduced me to a whole new world. I don't want it to end, but I know it has to.

"Now I'm going to stop talking. It's late, and you need your sleep so you can remove that last tree in the morning. It exhausts me just to think about all the work you've done. Thank you for everything."

She rolled over onto her other side, sending him the message that she would leave him alone.

Stifling a groan, he turned off the heater and shut off the engine before lowering his seat all the way back. This was the second conversation they'd had where she'd admitted wanting to stay longer. To keep her here was all he'd been able to think about. But until he had answers about Jenny, he couldn't beg Alex to stay in Whitebark, let alone offer her more.

If Mr. Derrick's private investigator couldn't find Jenny, then Wyatt felt he could put that aspect of his past away. Maybe he'd need psychiatric help to do it, but at least he'd approached the attorney about an impossible situation. While he willed himself to fall asleep, he determined to phone Mr. Derrick after they reached the ranch.

The next time he became aware of his surroundings, he heard a woman's scream and realized it was Alex. Next he heard Fluffy's *baa*. She reached across the console and clung to him. "Something huge knocked against my window just now."

"I'll check outside."

"No—don't—"

He chuckled. "Don't worry. I'll be fine."

Wyatt climbed out of the cab and reached for the lantern. When he turned it on, he saw animal footprints around the truck. A smile broke the corners of his mouth. His watch said four in the morning. He turned out the lantern and put it on top of the truck. After he got back inside, he pulled Alex to him—the console made it difficult.

"Judging by the size of the footprints, a big bull moose has been hanging around. He probably smelled Fluffy. No doubt his antlers knocked against your window by accident while he was snooping, but Fluffy sounded the alarm to save you and now it's gone."

Her face had nestled in his neck. "You think that's what she did?"

"It makes a good story to tell Grandad."

"Oh, Wyatt—" She laughed nervously and lifted

her head to look at him. Their mouths were only an inch apart. "I was frightened to death."

"But you're with me, so there's no need for you to worry."

"I know. That's why I reached for you and came close to strangling you. I'm sorry to have let out that terrified scream. It could have wakened the dead."

Her lips were too much for him to resist. "I'm not complaining," he admitted before covering her mouth with his own. It was there for the taking. He couldn't help himself. She was so warm and responsive, arousing his desire further.

She welcomed him with a hunger that couldn't be denied. Their growing attraction over several days and nights of being thrown together in the tent had made them insatiable.

"I've wanted to kiss you again. You have no idea how much," he admitted later, brushing her face and throat with his lips. "When Jose drove you up to the camp, I thought a golden-haired angel had alighted from his truck and my eyes were deceiving me."

She responded to him with a passion that made him feverish. "When I saw your picture over the fireplace, I couldn't wait to meet you. I need you to know these have been the most wonderful days and nights of my entire life. I'll never forget you."

"We haven't said goodbye yet," he murmured against her throat, dreading the moment that was coming.

"But we're going to have to." Her voice shook with emotions that were swamping him, as well.

"Let's not think about tomorrow. We have the rest of this night and I feel like devouring you."

"Wyatt—" The ache in her voice was all he needed to hear.

Despite the console, they ended up communicating with every kind of kiss and caress imaginable until early light filtered through the trees, bringing the morning. After a final, thorough kiss, he sat back to stare at her.

"Don't look at me like that," she begged him. "I haven't seen a mirror in days."

"A woman as stunning as you doesn't need one. I'm glad you can't look at yourself."

"Why?"

"Because my beard has given you a rash. When we get back to the ranch, my grandfather's going to know what we've been doing."

A smile broke out on her face. "It'll make his day."

"You're right about that."

She lifted those fabulous green eyes to him. "Maybe we could stay here for another twenty-four hours before we have to go home?"

"I'm all for it, but we're down to two cans of Vienna sausages and dried apricots for breakfast. How does that sound?"

"Like heaven."

"I think we're already there." He drew her into his arms once more and kissed her until they heard Fluffy's cries.

Wyatt buried his face in her hair. "Our ewe feels neglected. She knows you're in here with me and she doesn't like it. Something tells me I'm going to have a big problem on my hands after we get to the ranch and you leave. Jose will have his work cut out keeping her happy."

"How long will it take you to dismantle your camp and come back down?"

"That all depends. From two to three days, maybe more."

"Is Pali expecting you to go right back up?"

"I'm afraid so. We don't want to be caught in another blizzard."

"Of course not." A huge sigh escaped her. "Your work is never done." She raised her seat to a sitting position. The intimacy they'd shared during the early morning hours was over. It pained him, but he adjusted his own seat, as well.

"That's not true, but right now I'd like to get the tree moved. We'll finish off our food on the way down to the ranch. Fluffy will be glad for a bed in the barn. When she's settled, I'll cook up a storm for our lunch while you enjoy a long hot shower."

"Then it will be your turn while I do the dishes."

"Grandad will badger you the whole time, wanting to know everything. Let's hope you have something to cover that rash," he said before climbing out of the cab with his gloves.

Alex watched the man she adored get busy attaching the cable to the tree trunk. She took advantage of the time to get out and make a stop behind some trees. When she saw the animal prints in the snow, she realized Wyatt hadn't been exaggerating about the size of the moose that had visited them during the night.

After getting in the back of the truck, she patted Fluffy's head. "Thanks for warning us last night." The sheep let out a *baa*. It touched Alex's heart. She fed her some crackers. "We're going home. Maybe Jose will bring in another ewe so you'll have a friend with you. I'll ask Wyatt. See you in a little while."

WYATT WINCHED THE tree trunk out of the way. Then he opened the sausages and apricots for them to eat.

Her green eyes smiled into his. "This is delicious."

Alex's sunny nature was a miracle to him. "A step up from the K rations soldiers had to eat during the war."

"Well, I agree I'd rather eat this than corned mutton or Pali's blood sausage."

After chuckling, he drank half a bottle of water and turned on the engine. In a few minutes they'd left the trees. The valley lay below with snow already a day old. Twenty minutes later they reached the ranch. As he pulled around the side of the house, he knew that his world had changed forever.

The incredible woman sitting at his side had brought him back to life during the raging storm of the decade. She'd made him believe all things were possible. Kissing her this morning had brought out longings he'd thought had died when Jenny went away.

He turned to her. "We're home."

No sooner had he said the words than Jose came

out of the house and walked up to his side of the truck. Wyatt put the window down. "Hey, Jose."

The foreman smiled at them. "I'm glad you're back. Your grandfather was worried and wanted me to go up for you. I was just about to load the horses. Yours needs the exercise."

"I agree, but there's no need for that now. We brought back a ewe with a broken leg. If you would help me settle her in the barn, I'd be grateful. Her name is Fluffy."

A puzzled look broke out on his face. "Fluffy?"

"She's Ms. Dorney's new pet."

Jose laughed, then said, "You've had a dozen calls while you were gone. The most important one was from a Mr. Derrick. He phoned and told me it was urgent that you get back to him as soon as possible."

Wyatt's adrenaline surged. "How long ago was that?"

"Three days, maybe."

"Thanks. I'll call him."

He turned to Alex who'd heard that conversation. "Let's go inside and I'll show you to the guest bedroom with its own bathroom."

"I can't wait.

Wyatt got out of the cab and reached for her two cases in the back seat. She followed him into the house and he led her down the hall to one of the guest rooms. He put her cases on the carpeted floor. "Make yourself comfortable."

Her eyes clung to his. "It sounds like you might have news about Jenny."

He sucked in his breath. "Maybe." All he wanted to do at this moment was crush her in his arms, but he couldn't do that. Not right now. "I'll be back soon."

Tearing himself away, he walked to the living room where he found his grandfather watching TV. Otis got up and ran over to him. He patted the dog. "Hiya, boy. How are you, Grandad?"

"Wyatt!" The older man's eyes teared.

"Don't get up." Wyatt gave him a hug.

"Where's Alex?"

"In the guest room taking a shower. I have to go outside and take care of a ewe with a broken leg. Jose's going to help me. Then I'll fix lunch and we'll tell you everything."

"Martha made lunch and I've already eaten. I'm sure there's enough for you and Alex."

"I'll check."

"Thank God you're both home safe. How's Pali?"

"Indestructible."

Wyatt squeezed his grandfather's shoulder before hurrying back out to the truck. Between him and Jose, they transported the ewe to one of the empty stalls. Jose had already put down fresh hay and a bucket of water.

They finished making Fluffy comfortable before Wyatt slipped back into the house and hurried to his bedroom. After stripping, he showered and shaved in record time, then threw on his robe and sat on the side of the bed to make the call. The secretary told him to hold. Too restless to sit still, he got to his feet and paced the floor.

"Mr. Fielding?"

"Yes, Mr. Derrick. I just got back from being in the mountains."

"Well, I'm glad you called me back. I have news. Jenny Allen had her name legally changed in court five years ago. She's now Rachel Brimley. She's still single and resides in San Francisco. She rents a modest apartment on Tehama Street and has worked for Hargrove and Adams, an advertising firm in the center of the city, for almost four years. Her parents live in Flagstaff, Arizona, in a community where her father teaches in a church."

Wyatt's eyes closed tightly. "Does she have any idea I'm looking for her?"

"No. The investigator traced her there. I'll email you her address. The rest is up to you. If you decide to talk to her, then all your questions will be answered."

"I'm indebted to you, Mr. Derrick. As soon as you send me your bill, I'll put a check in the mail."

"Thank you, and good luck."

He hung up the phone, amazed the attorney had found her and knew that much information, even about her family. After all these years he could get his questions answered, but he couldn't think right now. Not when Alex filled his mind and heart. The thought of her leaving Wyoming was tearing him apart.

After dressing in a long-sleeved Western shirt and

fresh jeans, he walked through to the living room and found Alex deep in conversation with his grandfather. She'd put on a silky blue blouse with a khaki wraparound skirt her figure did wonders for.

No more cowboy boots to hide her fabulous legs. He could smell the fragrance of her peach shampoo. This was the first time he'd seen her with lipstick, a pink frost that suited her skin to perfection. The rash was still obvious.

Her eyes darted to his. "I've been telling him all about Fluffy and the way she warned us that a moose was walking around the truck."

His grandfather looked at him without blinking, but he didn't fool Wyatt, who knew the older man had set up the whole thing and was hoping for a happily-ever-after story. "I take it you gave her the information she needed to write her article."

"I learned about lamb and a lot of other things I didn't know," she interjected with a grin. "Like how to operate a winch. He had to clear three trees from the trail in order for us to get down.

"More importantly, my boss will be delighted that my research came from an expert, Mr. Fielding. Wyatt told me he learned everything from you." That brought a smile to his grandfather's face. "I've already sent in a rough draft, and I'll send you an autographed copy of the magazine the second it's off the press."

Wyatt put his hands on his hips. Already he sensed a change in her. He didn't like what he was thinking because it sounded like a goodbye speech.

"I found out she's got a lot of courage and forti-tude for an Easterner, Grandad."

The older man looked at both of them. "What are your plans now?"

"I called my parents and they're anxious for me to get home, so I already booked my flight to JFK. It leaves at seven in the morning from Jackson Hole."

Wyatt knew it!

"I also reserved a hotel room for tonight at the Antler Inn in Jackson and will arrange for a rental car so I can drive from Whitebark. That means I'll be leaving soon."

She might as well have knocked Wyatt's legs out from under him. "In that case, forget the rental car. I'll drive you to Jackson now and we'll eat on the way. Give me a minute to get the car out of the ga-rage."

By the look on his grandfather's face, he wasn't happy about the news, either. "You can't wait an-other day?"

"My parents were upset when I didn't get home on schedule. They've made plans for the family. I have to go, but I'll never forget this visit. I'm indebted to you and your grandson."

She gave him a kiss on the cheek, then turned to Wyatt. "I'll bring my suitcase out."

He nodded. "Meet me in front. See you in a while, Grandad."

Wyatt left the house and walked to the garage to back out his dark blue Chrysler sedan. He made a circle and drove in front where he found Alex waiting. After getting out to put her bags in the back seat, he helped her in and they drove out to the main road.

The snowplows had cleared the streets. All the recent snow would remain until spring. He stopped at Hilda's, the drive-through he and the other firefighters always went to on their way home from a fire.

"I know you're starving. Let's eat now."

She nodded. "I'd like a hamburger, fries and coffee. But I know it won't be as good as the brew we drank at the camp."

"Nothing's that good."

He put in their order. While they waited, she phoned the rental car company and canceled her request. After she hung up she looked at him.

"Did you call that attorney?"

"Yes."

Alex averted her eyes. "Sorry. I shouldn't have asked."

"It's all right."

"No. It's not. You don't have to tell me anything."

He drove to the window and picked up their food. Afterward, he parked in one of the stalls while they ate. "I've found out where she lives, what she's doing and that she's still single. She's also going by a different name, but I'm assuming she doesn't want her parents to know where she is, or she's hiding from someone. I still haven't decided what I want to do about it."

"Does your grandfather know?"

"I never told him I hired an attorney. At this point,

I'm not sure I want to tell him anything. It would only worry him more."

She remained silent while they ate. Once they'd finished, he pulled out onto the main road and headed for the freeway. Soon they were on their way to Jackson. Traffic wasn't too heavy, and the drive was pleasant under a sunny sky.

"What can I do to help you, Wyatt?"

"Not a thing, but thank you for asking."

A troubled sigh escaped her. "I can't even imagine how you must be feeling right now. I'm weighed down with guilt that you're driving me to the airport, the last thing you want to do. You never asked for me to show up at your sheep camp uninvited. After all this time, you're still taking care of me because that's the kind of man you are.

"I'd give anything to repay you, but I don't know how. Even if I did figure something out, you'd refuse it. All I have are words to thank you."

"They're enough."

Wyatt turned on the radio and they listened to the news. Before long he pulled into the covered area outside the lobby of the Antler Inn. He helped her out of the car with her bags. The knowledge that he'd found Jenny had put a barrier between them and they both knew it.

How ironic that during the night he'd spent hours kissing the daylights out of Alex, but since then the situation had changed. He needed to uncomplicate his life one way or another before things went any further with her.

He walked her inside to the desk to make certain she got her key card. Then he followed her to the elevator.

"Alex—"

She shook her head and refused to look at him. "Don't come any farther or say another word. What we had together I'll always cherish. Go home to your grandfather and your life, Wyatt. I'll hold every good thought of you, no matter what happens."

She entered the elevator with her bags and the doors closed, freezing him out.

This was hell in a new dimension.

He didn't sleep that night.

Needing to move fast, he left for the Jackson airport the next morning to fly to San Francisco.

Telling his grandfather that he had to go out of town on business overnight and wouldn't be back until the next evening, he promised to explain the reason upon his return.

Jose and Martha would be in charge while he was gone. Pali wouldn't be alarmed if Wyatt didn't make it back to the camp for a few days.

Once Wyatt arrived in San Francisco, he checked into the Ramada Limited Hotel near the airport. It was one in the afternoon when he reached his room and used the hotel phone to call Hargrove and Adams Advertising. A receptionist answered.

"May I speak with Ms. Brimley?" Eleven years ago he would have given anything to have found out where her parents had sent her so he could go after her. It was a surreal moment for him to realize he had finally caught up to her.

"She's with a client but should be available in about ten minutes."

"In that case, I'll call back in a little while. Thank you."

He'd accomplished his first objective. She was at work. Wyatt hung up before the receptionist could get any more information from him. She would tell Jenny who would see the caller ID and know the call had come from the hotel. If she was curious, she would try to find out who'd been trying to reach her.

When he didn't get a call back within an hour, he decided to take a taxi to her work. At least she'd been alerted that someone had tried to talk to her before he showed up at her office. This was it. After eleven years, this was the moment Wyatt had been waiting for.

Chapter Eight

Alex's parents picked her up outside the airline terminal at JFK on Tuesday afternoon and they drove home to New Jersey. It was wonderful to see them. She told them everything that had happened from the time she'd rented the car and driven to Whitebark until her return to Jackson Hole yesterday.

But the pain of leaving Wyatt was so great, her mother picked up on it right away. The second they entered the house, she put her arm around Alex. "You're not yourself. Tell us what's wrong, honey."

Her father followed them into the family room where they sat down on the couch. His eyes were filled with concern. "We want to help you."

Tears spilled down her cheeks. "I love you both so much, but no one can fix what's wrong."

Her mother gripped her hand. "You can tell us anything, no matter how terrible."

"I've fallen in love with the most wonderful man in existence, but I'm pretty sure I'll never see him again."

"You're talking about Wyatt Fielding, of course. Did he tell you he loves you, too?" her father asked.

"No, Dad. We got close, but he's not in the same place I am emotionally. We didn't make plans to see each other again."

Her mother hugged her. "He must be exceptional to have affected you like this."

"Wyatt's so fantastic you can't imagine. Somehow I'm going to have to find a way to survive without him in my life, but I don't know how. I—I've taken a lot of pictures of him and the camp with my phone." Her voice faltered.

She pulled it out of her purse and scrolled through the gallery of photos. "This one is my favorite. It shows him carrying the injured ewe through the snow with Pali. He was so tender with her."

She let her mother and father look at it, but they didn't stop at one picture. "Look at all that snow!" her mom exclaimed. "How high up in the mountains were you?"

"Seven thousand feet. He and Pali brought the sheep down from the ten-thousand-foot level. They work so hard! Most people wouldn't be able to handle it."

Her father smiled. "It doesn't look like hard work has hurt him any."

"Not at all. He fights fires in his spare time and runs the ranch, plus cares for his grandfather. There's a picture of him in his firefighter dress uniform. Let me find it." She scrolled until she found it. "I took this from the photo his grandfather had put on the mantel."

Both her parents studied it. Her mother looked

up at her first. "The physical attraction is no longer a mystery. Good heavens!"

"That's what I thought the moment I laid eyes on him," she admitted. "He's gorgeous beyond description."

"Gorgeous and hardworking," her father murmured. "That's quite a combination. Are you ready to tell us why he's not emotionally where you are, or is it too difficult to talk about?"

She got up from the couch and looked down at them. "It's a very sad story."

"We'd like to hear it, honey." Her dad's compassion broke her down.

Taking a deep breath, she unloaded on them about Jenny. About the miscarriage. Alex told them everything.

"When we pulled in to the ranch yesterday, the foreman told Wyatt the attorney he'd hired to investigate her whereabouts had called. Wyatt was to return the call ASAP.

"I knew it meant that she'd either been found, or that she'd disappeared and could never be found. In either case, I could see the phone call had sent Wyatt into shock. Certainly it changed everything for me. I knew then I had to leave."

After she finished talking, her father stood up and put an arm around her. "You were wise to come home, even if it tore you apart. The man does need time to work things out."

"I realized that, but you have no idea how hard it

was to leave. His grandfather didn't want me to go. He's a darling. I took pictures of him, too."

"I admit that knowing how much you love him, I'm surprised you didn't stay a little longer."

Alex looked at her mother. "I could have, but after what happened with Ken, I learned my lesson."

Her mom got to her feet. "What lesson?"

"The one I never admitted to you. It was too embarrassing at the time."

"We're listening, honey," her father said.

"When I told you I thought he'd met another woman, though I had no concrete proof, that was only part of the reason I broke our engagement."

"What other reason was there?"

"The truth is that he said something that cut me to shreds. Since then, I realized it was his immaturity talking." In the next breath, she repeated what Ken had said to her.

Pained expressions broke out on their faces.

"That night I realized I needed to make my own life and not depend on any man. If nothing else, when I left Whitebark yesterday I had Wyatt's respect. It's the one thing that will have to help me survive from here on out. But I can tell you this. There'll never be another man for me. Wyatt has all of my heart and soul forever."

With tears gushing from her eyes, she ran to her bedroom and threw herself across the bed. The sobs came until oblivion took over.

WHEN WYATT REACHED the advertising firm, the receptionist asked him to be seated and she'd tell Ms.

Brimley to come out. He reached for a business magazine and was reading it when Jenny appeared. She bore only a faint resemblance to the girl Wyatt had loved.

She'd put on ten to fifteen pounds and was attractive in a different way. She wore a fashionable ruffle-hemmed gray suit skirt and jacket with a scarf. She had a trendy short haircut and had dyed it a dark red. The color brought out her brown eyes.

Her ears were pierced. In her wedges, she seemed taller. Her parents wouldn't have tolerated anything she'd done to herself, but Wyatt approved. In fact, he felt tremendous relief to see how she'd gotten on with her life so far and had made a success of it.

He stood up, drawing her attention.

Her face lost a little color. "Wyatt—*you're* the one who called here earlier?"

"It's been a long time. You look good Je—Rachel. Is there a place where we can talk?"

She blinked, as if she couldn't believe what she was seeing. "Come back to my office."

He followed her past the curious receptionist and down a hall. She still walked the same. Some things didn't change.

"Please sit down." He did as she asked while she closed the door. Then she sat in the swivel chair behind her desk. "How did you find me?"

"About a month ago I hired an attorney who has a very efficient private investigator working for him. Yesterday I learned where he found you, so I came immediately."

After a long silence, she asked, "Did you ever try to find me before now?"

"Not after I went to your house and was told you'd gone away. Your parents made it clear they wouldn't be consenting to our marriage and that I wasn't to see you again. My grandparents advised me not to try to find you, that your parents were still legally responsible for you and they had a right to take you away."

Sadness crept into her eyes. "That was a nightmarish time. I needed you."

He could hardly swallow. "We both needed each other. Your losing the baby was something I'll never forget. What happened that night, Jenny?"

"It was over quickly. After my parents left the hospital, I phoned my best friend, Annie Walters. Remember her?"

"Of course."

"She knew everything about us and was the one who saved me."

"What do you mean?"

"I called her from my room and told her I had to get away from my parents. She borrowed her parents' truck and came to the hospital. Toward morning I sneaked out and we drove to Arapahoe."

"The reservation… That's the last place I would have thought of."

"Annie's very smart. She brought me a little money so I could stay overnight at the health-care center there. I had to wait for the bleeding to slow down before I could go anywhere."

"Annie never said a word to me."

"She didn't dare. She knew my parents, and for years had encouraged me to run away from home." Tears filled her eyes. "The only reason I didn't was because of you."

Her words compounded Wyatt's guilt. "What happened next?"

"I stayed in Arapahoe at a youth shelter for a month for free. I cut my hair and dyed it, praying my parents wouldn't find me. Annie came to visit me twice. On her last visit she brought me money and clothes and drove me to the bus station in Riverton. I bought a one-way ticket to San Francisco using my new name. Of course, it wasn't made legal for several years."

He shook his head. "How did you survive?"

"I went directly to the YWCA and got involved in a teen program for homeless girls like me. At eighteen I applied for work at a restaurant washing dishes. Thus began a series of jobs until I'd made enough to go to college and rent an apartment. I've saved enough money to pay Annie back, but I don't know where to send it. I don't want her parents to know."

"That's something I can do for you. Please."

"Thank you, but it's something I have to do. I'll find a way."

"You shouldn't have had to go through that, Jenny. I would have done anything for you."

"I know. But my parents hated you because I loved you. They're sick people and still are. Something is terribly wrong with them."

"I agree. Do you know where they are?"

"No. I never want to know."

Then Alex would never hear it from him. "I can't get over how strong you are."

A smile broke out on her face. "I got help and I love my job. I have good friends."

"That makes me happier than you'll ever know. Is there a man in your life now?"

"There's one guy, but it's not serious yet."

"I find that hard to believe. You've grown into a lovely woman."

"Thank you. I've met several men, but in all honesty none of them compare to you. Seeing you now, I can tell you've thrived since high school. How are your grandparents?"

"I lost my grandmother a couple of years ago. Grandad is as well as can be expected. He's hard of hearing now and has a limp from a hunting accident."

"I'm sorry. Are you still herding sheep for him?"

"Yes, and fighting fires in my spare time."

"Wow. You always were amazing, but I don't see a ring on your finger. How come?"

Tell her the truth. She deserves it.

"I've met someone, but don't know where it's going yet. Recently I decided it was time to find you if I could and learn what happened. I need to talk about the baby. Did the doctor tell you if it was a boy or a girl?"

"It was too early to tell," she whispered.

Wyatt moaned. "Our child would be ten by now."

"Yes, but I try not to think about it because it hurts too much."

"I know what you mean. What can I do for you? I'd like to help you financially."

She shook her head. "No, Wyatt. I'm doing fine. What I want doesn't have to do with money. But I'll tell you this. Seeing you today has taken away the pain of wondering what happened to you. I remember that you lost your parents at five. I was afraid that when we were torn apart, it would bring back your nightmares. I'm so glad you came to see me today! In case you've forgotten, you always were the most handsome bull rider on the planet."

The old Jenny had come through for a moment.

"I was so crazy about you, I could never see anyone else. Come here, Jenny."

She walked around the desk and he wrapped her in his arms, rocking her for a long time. While he was immersed in new feelings and emotions, the phone rang on her desk. They broke apart and she answered it.

"I'm going to go so you can get on with business," he whispered.

"You're leaving?"

"I've got to get back to the ranch. Grandad has been neglected too long. Just remember that if you ever need anything, you know where to find me."

She nodded. "I do know. How could I ever forget?"

"Goodbye, Jenny."

As he started to leave, she called his name, though

she was still on the phone. "I might just come and see you."

Wyatt hadn't expected that comment, but he realized that coming to her work hadn't given her enough time to talk things out. He nodded and left her office to phone for a taxi.

If he hurried, he could make the last flight to Jackson this evening. The first thing he wanted to do was pay Annie back for her help. He'd had no idea she'd been involved. But since Jenny was pretty adamant that she wanted to be the one to pay Annie back, Wyatt realized it was her decision, not his.

During the flight home his mind went over Jenny's story. When he lost his parents and brother, he'd thought no one's life could be worse. But knowing what Jenny had been through with her parents made him realize there were different degrees of suffering.

ALEX RECEIVED A call from Mr. Goff on Wednesday morning. He asked her to come in to the office even though he'd told her to enjoy a week's vacation with her family.

Surprised that he wanted to see her, she rode the commuter train into the city. Since coming home Alex hadn't heard from Wyatt. She was in so much pain, she was hardly aware of what was going on around her.

Her boss sat back in his chair. "Alex? That's a dynamite rough draft you've turned in. I'm looking forward to reading the final one. It was virtually inspiring in parts."

"Thank you."

"You have a nose for uncovering trends and have been on the mark every time. It prompts me to ask if you'd consider accepting a new position here at the magazine."

She stared for a moment in shock. She'd been expecting her next assignment and had dreaded the thought of going anywhere. "You mean…a staff position?"

"Exactly. The magazine is doing better than ever and we're enlarging circulation. I'd like you to be one of our feature editors. Certain writers will report to you and you'll oversee their work. Would that appeal to you?"

Before Alex had gone to Wyoming, she would have said yes without thinking about it. But everything had changed since Wyatt had come into her life, paralyzing her ability to make decisions.

"I…don't know what to say."

"You'll be on salary with vacation and a benefits plan." He mentioned a salary she hadn't anticipated.

"Please don't think I'm not grateful for your faith in me, but this has taken me by surprise. Could I have some time to think about it?"

If he was bewildered over her answer when anyone else would have been overjoyed and grabbed at it, he was very decent about it. "I'll give you until next Wednesday, a week from today. How does that sound?"

"More than generous."

"Then enjoy this vacation time, because if you

decide to take the position, you'll be busy like never before."

"I believe it." Staying too busy to think was the only thing she could imagine doing to get through the rest of her life. "Thank you for the opportunity. I'll get back to you, Mr. Goff."

AFTER GETTING IN late following his return home from San Francisco, Wyatt got up the next morning and phoned his primary physician. Could he recommend a therapist he could talk to ASAP? Alex's departure had brought on such acute pain, he knew he couldn't live without help any longer.

His doctor got hold of a therapist in Riverton who agreed to fit him in that day as a favor. Wyatt said he'd be there. Relieved to get an appointment so fast, he hurried down to the kitchen to fix breakfast for himself and his grandfather.

"You say you saw Jenny for the first time yesterday?" the older man asked in a shaken voice.

"That's right. I hired an attorney last month and his private investigator found her in San Francisco."

The older man reached out to grasp Wyatt's arm. "How did it go?"

Wyatt told him everything he could.

"What are your feelings at this point?"

"Relief, gratitude."

"What else?" his grandfather prodded. "Are you going to see her again?"

Wyatt knew the older man not only wanted to know a lot more, but that he was dying to talk about

Alex, too. However, Wyatt wasn't ready for that discussion yet.

"I'm afraid that's a loaded question. It's why I have an appointment with a therapist in Riverton later today. I need to leave now. Jose and Martha will be here for you while I'm gone."

"Don't worry about me. Thank God you've finally taken your grandmother's advice!"

"Better late than never, eh?" Wyatt got up and squeezed his shoulder. "I'll be back by evening and we'll talk some more."

"Pali must be expecting you by now."

"He rarely worries—you know that. I'll drive up early tomorrow to dismantle the camp. Unless there are more problems with the ewes, it won't take more than a few days. Then I'll be back."

"I love you, son."

"I love you, too, Grandad." His throat tightened, the emotions inside threatening to choke him. "In case I've never told you this before, you're the best father a son could ever have wished for."

The older man gripped his hand hard.

"Now I've got to get going."

On the way to Riverton, Wyatt phoned Cole and asked him to make inquiries for him about an address for Annie Walters. Wyatt wanted to get in touch with her. Wyatt, Jenny, Annie and Cole had been in high school together and all four loved the rodeo. Cole said he'd look into it the minute he had time.

At two in the afternoon Wyatt arrived in Riverton

for his appointment and was shown in to Dr. Nyman's office. They shook hands and he sat down.

"Your doctor in Whitebark asked if I couldn't see you sooner than six weeks. I was glad we had a cancellation to accommodate you today."

"I'm very appreciative, Dr. Nyman."

"I see from your medical history that you're a twenty-nine-year-old sheep rancher and firefighter. Not married. No children."

Wyatt would have had a child if the miscarriage hadn't happened… "That's right. I live with my grandfather and take care of him."

"Before we discuss why you're here, are you having health problems I should know about that are affecting you in any way?"

"None."

"No history with the military?"

"None."

"Do you take drugs?"

"Nothing like that."

"Problems with the law?"

Wyatt shook his head.

The doctor smiled. "Good. Now that we've gotten those necessary questions out of the way, why are you seeking help?"

Wyatt filled him in on everything that had happened, from his family's deaths to Jenny's miscarriage and disappearance to his recent reunion with her.

Dr. Nyman cocked his head. "After losing your family in Nebraska, your mind probably couldn't take losing this woman and your baby after knowing happiness again. It was a crime that you and Jenny weren't able to grieve together over your loss," he said. "Her parents forced you apart. That was an unconscionable cruelty you were both subjected to. But I'm pleased to hear that you finally made contact with her. From the sound of it, she has gotten on with her life just as you have. The fact that you've both triumphed is a miracle."

Wyatt nodded. "I admit I was relieved to see she had a great job and looked wonderful."

"Now that you've had time to think about it, did it make you want to be with her again, to explore what future you could have with her, now that her parents are no longer in the picture?"

He stirred in the chair. "No, but she indicated she might come and see me. I'm not sure why."

"Perhaps your visit to her didn't bring her closure. It was a surprise to her, and maybe she still needs to talk about it."

"That could be true. I went by her office in the middle of her workday, which didn't give her much time. But to be honest, I'm afraid that seeing her after all this time has only weighed me down with a different kind of guilt."

"Guilt?"

"For all these years I've suffered because I couldn't protect Jenny against her parents. But after seeing her again, I'm now feeling guilty because I've met another woman."

"When was this?"

"Last week." Wyatt proceeded to tell him about Alex's arrival at camp, how close they had become during her time there and how difficult it had been to say goodbye.

The doctor's brows lifted. "You're missing her?"

Wyatt let out a frustrated laugh and jumped to his feet. "You don't know the half of it."

"Is that what's tearing you up now, that you're in love with two women?"

"A part of me will always love Jenny."

"But?"

"But I'm *in* love with Alex!"

"Does Jenny know there's another woman?"

Wyatt rubbed the back of his neck. "No. There wasn't enough time to get into that kind of a conversation. I had to get back to work."

"After locating her and flying all that way, why didn't you make the time?"

He eyed the doctor who knew how to dig. "I guess it's because I'd just come from being with Alex. She was on my mind."

"Does Alex know you're in love with her?"

"I never said the words."

"Did you ask her not to fly back to New York?"

"No. She had a job to get back to and family waiting for her."

Dr. Nyman tapped his pen on the table. "That isn't why you didn't stop her."

Wyatt waited for the doctor to tell him what he already knew.

"It was because you were afraid to reach out.

After your history of losses, it's understandable. But you're no longer five years old and powerless. From here on out, the rest has to be up to you.

"Your grandfather made a last effort to help you. Sounds like he sent Alex up to your camp for a reason. He and your grandmother have always been there, nudging you in the right direction. But this is the one time in your life you're going to have to act on your gut instinct. If you don't take a risk, you'll end up tending sheep without the joy of love and family that includes a wife and children."

The doctor was right. But if he took the risk and Alex turned him down, would he be able to handle it?

"Much as I don't want to admit it, you're good, Dr. Nyman. I'll think about everything you've said. Thank you for fitting me in."

"You're welcome." The doctor smiled. "Make another appointment with my receptionist and I'll look forward to talking to you in our next session."

Wyatt left the doctor's office and headed back to the ranch knowing a decision had to be made about the direction of his life. He hoped like hell he wouldn't need another visit. As much as he liked Dr. Nyman and thought he was a good therapist, Wyatt didn't want to sit through a series of sessions. He wanted to make things happen.

Chapter Nine

Another week came and went for Alex. Now it was Wednesday. D-day. She needed to tell Mr. Goff if she would take the new position or not, but she wasn't anywhere near ready to make a decision. She'd wrestled with it during her vacation. Every day and night away from Wyatt had been agony. If anything, her pain was worse.

Her dad had gone to work that morning, but her mother had stayed home and made breakfast for the two of them.

"What are you going to do, honey?"

"I don't know. I'm going crazy. If Wyatt found Jenny and is still in love with her, then it's possible they're together now and that's why I haven't heard from him."

"Do you honestly think he could have shown you so much love up on that mountain if he's still in love with Jenny? I don't believe it, especially when they've been separated for so many years. I happen to believe the old saying that love has to be fed."

"I want to believe that, too."

Her mom sat back in the chair. "You don't know what's been going on since you left. I'm thinking it might be a good idea for you to go back to Wyoming and find out."

Alex's head shot up. "What?"

"You did leave awfully fast, without knowing what kind of news Wyatt had received. I think you should thank him in person one more time for all he did to keep you safe. Surely he'll tell you if he went to see Jenny and what happened between them. Knowing the truth is better than living like this, honey. At least you'll find out which way the wind is blowing so you can make decisions about your own life."

Alex frowned. "You don't think he would see me as a clingy, needy woman? Remember what I told you Pali said, that the women were always after Wyatt. That's why he liked going up in the mountains, to get away from them."

"Alex, as I recall, you told us Pali was a fun-loving man and enjoyed a good joke. I bet he was teasing you because he sensed right away you and Wyatt were attracted to each other. Who else knew him better?"

She blinked. "I don't know."

"Think about it. If Wyatt had thought you were too needy, he wouldn't have allowed himself to get involved with you while you were thrown together. He could have asked Pali to give up the camper for you until the storm was over. Did you ever consider that?"

"No."

"He certainly could have erected a separate tent for you so you'd get the message loud and clear that he wasn't interested."

"But, Mom, Wyatt kept those extra tents in case a sheep needed to be separated from the herd. He ended up having to use one of them for Fluffy."

Her mother smiled and shook her head. "Not all of them. You're in denial. From all you've told us, he didn't have an agenda like your former fiancé. Wyatt Fielding is the furthest thing from a cruel man. Remember—he isn't Ken."

That was what Wyatt had said to her.

"Honey?"

"Yes?"

"Since you told Wyatt you were the one who broke off your engagement, have you thought that maybe he's waiting for *you* to make the first move?"

Was he?

"What if he was hoping you wouldn't leave the second you reached Whitebark, but you did? And don't forget you said he told you he thought his grandfather had sent you up to the camp on purpose."

"Wyatt and I talked about that, and it did make sense."

"Apparently his grandparents feared the past had injured him and he would never find another woman or get married."

"Yes, but—"

"But what? Isn't it possible Wyatt is afraid you're avoiding contact because of what he said about his grandfather's agenda? What if Wyatt believes he did damage and is hoping you'll come back on your own because you love him, and for no other reason?"

Alex jumped up from the table. "If I thought that... Has Dad said anything to you about this?"

"Of course. Now that you've told us everything, he's in full agreement with me and wishes you hadn't come home at all."

"Oh, Mom—"

"Why don't you make an appointment to meet with Mr. Goff and tell him you can't give him an answer yet. Let him decide to take back the offer or not. Fighting for a great love is more important."

Alex ran around the table and hugged her mother so hard she was surprised she hadn't broken a rib. Then she reached for her phone to call the magazine office. Mr. Goff's secretary put her through to him.

"What's the verdict, Alex?"

"I'm so grateful to you, Mr. Goff, but I don't have an answer yet. I have to fly back to Wyoming for a few days first, so I'll understand if you give that position to someone else." She would show Wyatt the finished article, though it hadn't been published yet.

"I'm not in any hurry. But get back to me soon."

"That's so nice of you. I promise I'll phone you before long."

"That'll be fine."

Her heart started to hammer away at the thought of seeing Wyatt again.

WEDNESDAY NIGHT WYATT and Pali ate dinner in the camper. Wyatt had brought fresh provisions for them along with T-bone and salmon steaks on ice to enjoy over their last few days in the mountains. He'd taken his sleeping bag and bunked with Pali while they'd dismantled the camp. Now everything was loaded in Wyatt's truck. They'd vaccinated the herd of sheep, but it had taken two days longer than planned.

Pali eyed him with curiosity. "You've been restless ever since you got up here, Wyatt. I can tell you're anxious to go home tomorrow. What's going on with you?"

Wyatt finished off the last of his steak and sat back, studying Pali. Over the years, the two of them had confided in each other. No one was a better listener or friend. "I'm in love."

Pali laughed so hard Gip got to his feet and started barking. "That's not news, my friend, but it took you a hell of a long time to admit it. Does she know?"

"Not yet. I don't know if she's in love with me."

"You mean you're not sure? Come on—I knew it when she didn't ask if she could stay in another tent alone that first day. Her beautiful green eyes never left you."

"I didn't make it easy for her by telling her about Jenny. But I have news on that front. I had Jenny traced. Before I came up here, I learned where she's living and flew to San Francisco."

Pali's brows furrowed. "How did that go?"

"Better than I would have imagined." Wyatt told Pali the essence of their meeting. "We talked about the baby. I learned what I needed to know and it helped me more than you can imagine."

"Enough to put this behind you at last?"

He nodded. "I already have."

"I'm glad you've finally been able to close the cover on that book."

"Except I'm not sure it's completely closed yet."

"Why not?"

"Jenny said she might come and visit me."

Pali stared at him for a long time. "That's fine, but don't let the 'might' stop you from doing what you're dying to do."

"I won't. Alex is in my blood."

His friend smiled. "No news could make me happier. She's perfect for you. Have you heard from her since she left?"

"No. That's what's troubling me."

"But you're going to find out!"

Wyatt finished his coffee. "I'm flying to New York in the next few days." The visit to Dr. Nyman had galvanized him into action. If he wasn't needed at up here at camp, he'd have gone sooner.

"Good for you."

He flicked Pali a searching glance. "Speaking of news, I wish you had some for me." Wyatt knew Pali had met a woman named Saveria last Christmas and had spent time with her again when he'd gone home in the spring. He'd talked a lot about her.

"Maybe when I go back in December."

"I'll be hoping that works out. I want to come to your wedding."

A broad smile broke out on Pali's face. "I plan to dance at yours!"

THURSDAY MORNING WYATT waved to Pali and took off. Because the warm weather had been holding, he made it down the mountain through the remaining snow without any difficulties. During the trip his mind replayed the truck ride with Alex back to the ranch. He ached for her.

When he reached the forested area, it reminded him of those hours holding her in his arms and the breathtaking way she'd kissed him back. She loved him, all right. Even without the words, he knew it in every atom of his body. He'd felt it in the way she'd looked at him before the elevator doors had closed at the hotel in Jackson, taking her away from him.

What they'd shared during the blizzard had forced them together, sealing their fate. His grandfather's matchmaking had delivered a beautiful, special woman into his arms. Now it was up to Wyatt to convince Alex he couldn't live without her.

After parking near the back door of the ranch house, he hurried inside to check on his grandfather. After that he would start to unload everything. He drank from the faucet in the kitchen before walking to the living room where he heard voices.

Assuming it was Martha, nothing could have prepared him for the sight of Jenny sitting by his grandfather, dressed in jeans, cowboy boots and a becoming tan Western shirt—the kind of outfit she used to wear. They were chatting like there hadn't been eleven years since their last meeting.

His grandfather saw him before she did. "Wyatt— you're back! Look who has come to see you, son!"

Wyatt was looking, but he couldn't believe it. He'd only just started to straighten out his life. Pali had warned that he shouldn't let what Jenny had said about a possible visit prevent him from going after his heart's desire. But he hadn't really believed she'd meant what she said about making a trip out here. Not this soon anyway.

Jenny got up and darted him a smile. She was holding the framed picture of him in her hands. "I'm so glad you're back," she said in a breathless voice, sounding like the old Jenny. Wyatt was at a loss for words.

"I've been telling your grandfather about your surprise visit to my office. Since you and I didn't have nearly enough time to talk, I decided to fly here. With my short red hair, he didn't recognize me at first. We've been catching up on years of news."

"She's here for a few days," his grandfather explained. "When I found out she'd booked in at the Whitebark Hotel, I told her she could stay with us. She's put her suitcase in the guest bedroom and we're about ready to eat. Martha will be here any minute with lunch."

For the first time in ages, he was angry with his grandfather. Why had he taken over and invited her to stay with them? Surely he knew he was putting Wyatt in a difficult position. What did he hope would be accomplished? Wyatt knew for a fact his grandfather had taken a liking to Alex.

"I hope it's all right."

There'd always been a sweetness in Jenny. "Of

course it's all right," Wyatt murmured. "How did you get here?"

"I rented a car to drive to Whitebark. But it was having problems, so I turned it in and took a taxi here."

Wyatt needed a minute to think. "Why don't you come outside with me? I have to unload a few things and check on our latest patient in the barn. I brought her down from the camp. You can meet her."

"Her?" She put the picture back on the mantel and followed him through the house to the truck.

"Yes. One of the pregnant ewes broke a leg." He climbed onto the truck bed and lowered some bales of hay to the ground to take inside. Jose had been mucking out one of the horse's stalls and stopped to help him.

Jenny remembered Jose, but the foreman didn't recognize her with red hair. The three of them chatted for a minute, then went inside where they were met with a couple of *baas*. Jenny laughed in surprise.

Wyatt walked over to the stall. "Fluffy? Say hello to Jenny." When the ewe saw them, she put her head back down.

"You've given it a name?"

"Wyatt wouldn't do that," Jose answered with a grin. "It was the visitor from New York, Ms. Dorney." He scratched his head. "She got the ewe eating animal crackers right out of her hand. I never saw anything like it."

Thank you, Jose.

Wyatt hunkered down to check on her leg before

shooting Jose a glance. "You've taken good care of her. She looks like she's recovering just fine. I'll come out this evening to clean her stall."

Not anxious for Jose to do any more talking about Alex, he went back out to the truck and retrieved his duffel bag. He'd unload everything later. "Let's go in the house, Jenny," he said after jumping down. "I'll take a shower. Then we'll be able to eat and talk."

"That's exactly what I want to do. I spoke to my boss before I left. She knows my story and is aware you and I didn't have the time we needed when you came to the office. She's given me a few days off to be with you."

"She sounds like an understanding woman." His visit to New York would have to wait a while longer.

Wyatt carried his bag to the bedroom and pulled out his toiletries. He showered and shaved before putting on a navy pullover and jeans. The whole time he got ready, he pondered the real reason Jenny had come.

Seeing her just now had surprised him, but it didn't make him want to crush her in his arms and never let her go. If he'd needed proof that he was deeply in love with Alex, he had it now. The disappointment that it hadn't been Alex sitting there talking to his grandfather was still with him.

As he'd told the doctor, Jenny would always be the love of his past. But too many years of living had separated them. There'd been too many changes that had pushed them in different directions and the love they'd once shared couldn't be resurrected.

Wyatt wanted to believe that she'd come because she needed closure. Maybe that was what this was all about. He hoped so, because he didn't want to hurt her, not after everything they'd been through.

When he was ready, he walked through the house to the kitchen where Jenny sat next to his grandfather at the table. Martha had made the older man's favorite, meat loaf and mashed potatoes. Wyatt joined them and listened as Jenny recounted the details of that night at the hospital to his grandfather.

"You went through a terrible ordeal, honey. Why do you think your parents were so cruel?"

Her brown eyes darted to Wyatt. "They were keeping a secret, but I didn't learn about it until that night."

"What secret?" Wyatt asked in bewilderment.

"I found out I wasn't their daughter."

Wyatt's breath caught. "You're not serious." No wonder she'd told him she knew nothing of her parents' whereabouts and didn't want to know.

"It was a shock to me, too, but it explained why our relationship never seemed right to me. I learned that my mother's unmarried sister had given birth to me, but she was dying and asked my parents to raise me. It was all kept hush-hush and they moved from Hardin to Whitebark with me where no one knew them.

"But when the doctor told them I was having a miscarriage, they went into a rage at the hospital. They told me I was no good, just like my birth mother, who didn't know the name of the man who'd gotten her pregnant.

"The doctor told them they needed to leave and come back the next day when they'd calmed down. I was so happy they'd gone, you'll never know. I never wanted to see them again. The news had liberated me. My friend Annie helped me get away."

His grandfather patted her hand. "We can be thankful all that is behind you."

"Believe me, I am." She looked at Wyatt with beseeching eyes. "One of the reasons I flew here was to tell you the truth about my parents. I wanted to say something in the office, but I couldn't talk about it while I had a client on the phone."

"You don't need to explain anything to me, Jenny, but I have to admit it grieves me to know how those two treated you."

When Wyatt thought about it, though, he realized she was the one who'd left without telling him where she was.

"Don't worry about me, Jenny. I had my grandparents."

"I knew they would help you. As for me, I got therapy after living in San Francisco. During those talks I came to see that, though they were strict and unfeeling, they raised me here in Whitebark where you and I eventually met. Our senior year in high school was the happiest one of my life."

Until Wyatt had met Alex, he'd been able to say the same thing. "I've never forgotten and never will,

Jenny. Since we've finished eating, what do you say we take a ride? The horses need the exercise."

His grandfather nodded. "You two go on. You have a lot to talk about."

She smiled. "I haven't ridden much since those days."

"It'll be good for you."

"I'm sure you're right."

Wyatt got to his feet. "It's warm out, but you'll still need a jacket."

"I'll get it and meet you at the barn." She stood up and gave his grandfather a kiss on the cheek before hurrying to the guest bedroom.

Wyatt and his grandfather stared at each other. "Can you beat that?"

"No, Grandad. She's a remarkable woman to have survived such a difficult beginning."

"It's good to see her again. She told me she has close friends. But it's too bad her birth mother died. The poor girl doesn't have family."

He was reading Wyatt's mind. "I'm just thankful she has a terrific job."

"She was telling me about it."

"Grandad, are you going to be all right if we go riding for an hour?"

"What do you think?"

Wyatt squeezed his shoulder and left the house through the back door. He found Jenny checking out the horses. "Have you decided which mount you want?"

"How about the bay?"

"She's a well-behaved mare."

Jenny followed him into the tack room. "You still have my old saddle!"

She remembered.

"It's all yours."

"Thank you."

"Do you need my help?"

"I don't know. We'll have to wait and see."

Of course she hadn't forgotten anything. She'd done a lot of riding with him. Soon their horses were bridled and saddled. His gelding, Rango, was excited to leave the barn. Most of the snow had melted.

How strange it felt to be out riding with Jenny and not feel the thrill of being with her. Unfortunately, more guilt descended because he wished it were Alex riding with him. His grandfather's last comment didn't help and had struck a nerve. *The poor girl doesn't have family.*

They made a wide circle around the property. Again and again his eyes went to The Winds where he'd spent the most exciting days and nights of his life falling in love with Alex.

"Wyatt? Jose said it was a woman from New York who named your patient Fluffy. How did that happen?"

"She's a writer for a food magazine. A couple of weeks ago she came to Wyoming to do research about the lamb industry. I gave her an interview. When she saw that the ewe had a broken leg, she felt sorry for her and called her Fluffy." He tried not to smile just remembering that moment.

"Where is she now?"

"Back in New York. Why do you ask?"

"When you came to my office and I told you I didn't see a ring on your finger, you didn't really answer my question. I just wondered if that woman is someone important to you."

There had to be total honesty between them. "She is."

"I thought maybe that was the case."

He reined in his horse. "She's the first woman I've been interested in since you disappeared from my life. After what you and I shared, I haven't been the same."

"Neither have I," she confessed.

"Jenny? Are you sorry I found you and came to see you?"

"At first I wasn't sure how I felt. After you left, I did a lot of soul-searching. All these years I've consoled myself that you loved me and that we would have gotten married and maybe had another baby if the circumstances had been different. I began to feel it was enough to have known our kind of love."

Wyatt related to everything she was saying. "But then I showed up," he interjected.

She nodded. "It wasn't like I'd thought it would be. Only in my dreams did I imagine that one day we'd meet and fall into each other arms, ready to take up where we left off. But the reality fell short. It brought up a lot of old feelings and the longing to be loved like that again."

He nodded. Their meeting had lacked the fire

they'd felt as teens. And spending time with her like this hadn't rekindled it.

"Shall we ride back and have a game of cards with my grandfather? He'd love that. Then we'll get dressed up. For old time's sake I'd like to take you to dinner at the hotel."

She smiled. "That's something we never did before."

"Not at the hotel. I never had the money, and we didn't want word to get back to your parents where we'd been. I'll race you to the barn."

"You're on!"

Chapter Ten

Late afternoon the same day, Alex's plane touched down at the Jackson Hole Airport. She'd arranged for a rental car ahead of time, so it was easy to drive directly from the airport to Whitebark. At ten after eight that evening, she checked in at the Whitebark Hotel and went straight to her room on the second floor.

It felt wonderful to shower and change into a new long-sleeved dark red sweater and black wool skirt. Her last meal had been on the plane and she was hungry, but Wyatt was continually on her mind.

No matter how she decided to get in touch with him, it wouldn't be through his grandfather. She didn't want Wyatt thinking his grandfather had manipulated anything this time. And as her mother had said, Wyatt needed to know she'd come on her own because she loved him.

Tonight he could be up on the mountain with Pali or out fighting fires with his crew. For that matter, he could be home with his grandfather or...

Wyatt could be with Jenny now. But if that had

happened, she needed to find out. Alex had come all this way to tell him how she felt and wouldn't be leaving until she'd learned the truth from him about his feelings.

While she ate dinner in the main restaurant downstairs, she composed her text to him, choosing her words carefully.

Hi, Wyatt. I hope you're well. How's Fluffy? I turned in my article and hope to give you a copy soon, but I thought you'd like to know my boss liked it a lot!

She didn't add that Mr. Goff had offered her a promotion and a new position if she wanted it. That could come later, depending on Wyatt's response to this text.

I told him I owed all my thanks to you. If you'd like an advance copy, I have one for you. I'd love to know what you think!

Alex decided she'd written enough but would wait to send the text until she'd gone back up to her room to be sure she'd said everything she wanted with no changes.

She got up from the table, but the crowded room made it difficult to walk freely. It seemed like every table was occupied. Approaching the cashier counter, she almost bumped into a couple coming her way. When she looked up, her legs came close to buckling.

"Wyatt—"

There he was, larger than life, wearing a tan Western suit and darker brown shirt. She noticed the head of every female in the room turn in his direction. With that wavy black hair and those rugged features, you couldn't look anywhere else.

He wasn't alone. At his side was a lovely red-headed woman in a trend-setting floral-print midi dress that left her shoulders bare. Something told her it had to be Jenny.

His penetrating blue eyes zeroed in on her in disbelief. A nerve pulsed at the corner of his mouth.

"*Alex*—I don't believe it. When did you arrive?"

"A couple of hours ago."

He rubbed his neck in a gesture she'd seen from him before. "Why didn't you tell me you were coming?"

"I wanted to surprise you."

"Are you checked in here?"

She nodded.

He turned to his companion. "Let me introduce you two. This is Rachel Brimley. She works for an advertising agency in San Francisco. Rachel, this is Alex Dorney who writes for a food magazine in New York."

Who? Alex was getting more confused by the minute. Was Wyatt seeing someone he hadn't mentioned? "How do you do."

"It's very nice to meet you," the other woman responded.

Alex looked at Wyatt, trying to keep her wits. "Speaking of the magazine, it hasn't been published yet. But I brought a copy of the final article with me. I'd love to hear what you think about it."

His eyes burned a hot blue. "I'll phone you."

"Good night."

Alex had purposely said good-night rather than goodbye to let him know she wasn't leaving town yet. She'd come to Whitebark for answers and wouldn't leave without them.

She made her way to the counter to pay her bill. Her hand was trembling so hard, the man taking her credit card gave her a second glance. While he did the transaction, she watched Wyatt and the other woman talking.

Though he didn't hold her arm, there was something deferential about the way he treated her. Alex couldn't remember the last time she'd known this kind of jealousy. She hadn't thought it was in her nature, but she'd been wrong.

Pali had warned her that women didn't leave Wyatt alone. What was a woman in advertising from San Francisco doing here in Whitebark? Did Wyatt have women from other states dropping in on him every week? Did he intend to keep on dating other women and forget the past?

When the cashier returned her card, she left the restaurant and hurried up to her room, but she was still shaking. Alex had left a copy of her article on the table next to the bed. On the flight out here, she'd thought of several ways to present it to him, never dreaming it would be here at the hotel in front of a woman he was taking out to dinner. But she'd mentioned it to him, and now she had to follow through and wait for his call.

For the rest of the evening she watched TV in her robe on top of the bed without taking anything in. At ten thirty she sat up and reached for her phone to text her parents and let them know that she'd arrived safely. That was when she noticed the text message she hadn't sent to Wyatt. She deleted it.

Maybe Rachel was staying at this hotel, too. If Wyatt was spending the night with her, he might not phone Alex before tomorrow. Because of his courtesy, she knew he'd get back to her when he could, so the only thing for her to do was wait. But it was going to be the longest night of her life imagining him kissing the other woman the way he'd kissed her.

WYATT LOOKED AT JENNY, who pressed on his arm. "I've changed my mind about eating dinner and know you have, too," she said. "Before we say goodnight, I want you to know that I'm flying back to San Francisco tomorrow."

He led her out to the foyer, his thoughts reeling. "Why so fast?"

"For the simple reason that coming here has proven to me we can never recapture what we had in our teens. When you left my office the other day, I was horribly confused and knew I had to see you again. But this visit has cleared up everything for me."

"What do you mean?" His heart was thundering in his chest.

"A few minutes ago, I saw you and Alex staring at each other. I recognized the look of love. It was written all over both of you. It was the look that was missing when we met in my office. But I flew here anyway, to be absolutely sure. Now I am. You need to be with *her*, so don't deny it."

Wyatt couldn't deny it. No matter how late the hour, before he went to bed tonight, he'd phone her. "What about our plans for tomorrow?"

"They don't matter."

"Of course they do. I insist on driving you to Arapahoe in the morning. I want to thank the people at the shelter there and make a contribution since I wasn't able to do anything for you at the time. They saved your life." .

"But those people won't be there after this long a time."

"It doesn't matter. The fact that the shelter exists means they're saving other girls' lives." He covered her hand. "Because of them, you were able to recover from the miscarriage. I would have given anything to help you through that experience."

Her eyes misted over. "I believe you've suffered more than I have."

He took a deep breath before letting her go. "I know that's not true. But I was haunted because I'd lost my brother so early in life and missed him. When you realized you were pregnant, I envisioned being a father to our child.

"I'm afraid I didn't express it enough how excited I was to know we were going to be parents. I could picture us teaching our boy or girl to ride and fish, to hike The Winds and camp out."

Jenny nodded. "When I started bleeding, my parents drove me to the hospital. The doctor examined me and said I'd lost the baby and the hospital would take care of it. I couldn't believe it. All our dreams...

"He asked me why I hadn't come in to see him before then. I explained that I was afraid of my parents and didn't want them to know. I'll always be grateful he helped me by telling them to leave."

Wyatt had heard enough. "Thank God that's in the past. Come on. Let's get you back to the ranch. I'd like to get an early start on the two-and-a-half-hour drive to Arapahoe in the morning."

He walked her out to his car and they drove home. Wyatt was relieved his grandfather had gone to bed. They walked down the hallway past his room to her door.

"I'm thankful you came, Jenny." He meant it. "Your visit has given us the time that was snatched away."

"It has helped me, too. I needed to see you again in order to give myself permission to fall in love a second time in my life. I told you there's a man I've been involved with, but I hadn't allowed it to become serious because he doesn't know about my past. I never let it go, and I'm afraid I've hurt him. But this visit has freed me. When I go back, I'm ready to tell him everything and see what happens."

He hugged her hard. "You couldn't have given me better news. You'll always have a place in my heart."

"And you in mine. When we leave in the morning, I'll say goodbye to your grandfather and bring my bags. That way you can drive me to Jackson Hole from Arapahoe. It'll save time for both of us." She eased herself out of his arms. "We need to get on with our lives. She's waiting for you, Wyatt."

He nodded. It was still unbelievable Alex was here. "You have to know I want you to find happiness, Jenny."

"It's all I ever wanted for you, too. Good night."

"Get a good sleep." Putting his hands on her shoulders, he kissed her forehead.

She shut the door. The click reminded him that their painful past was over.

As he started back down the hall, his grandfather opened his bedroom door. "I heard voices and need to talk to you before you go to bed."

Wyatt needed to talk to Alex before he did anything else, but he heard the seriousness in his grandfather's voice. "I have to go upstairs for a minute, but I'll be back."

He reached the foyer and took the stairs two at a time to his bedroom on the second floor. He tossed his suit jacket on the bed along with his cell phone and changed into his sweats. Then he sat down on the side of the bed to phone Alex. She wouldn't be asleep.

She answered on the second ring. "Wyatt?"

He closed his eyes tightly for a minute. To hear her voice sent his pulse racing. "Nothing could have surprised me more than seeing you tonight."

"I didn't expect to see you, either. I'd planned to phone you in the morning. I'm sorry you feel you have to call me now when I know you're with that other woman. I brought up the magazine in front of her so—"

"I know exactly why you did it," he broke in on her. "You were trying to make it easier for me to explain to Rachel how we knew each other. But it wasn't necessary. Rachel isn't a girlfriend, but I don't have time to explain until I see you tomorrow evening. Until then, I'll be out of town. Promise me you'll stay in Whitebark, Alex. I should be back by seven and will come to the hotel for you."

After a silence she said, "I'm not going anywhere."

"Do you swear you'll stay put?"

"Do you really have to ask me that?" she asked in troubled voice. "I would think that after what we went through, you would trust me by now."

"Not after the hasty exit you made back to New York the day we came down from the mountain. I got the impression you couldn't get away from me fast enough."

"That's not true!" she fired back.

"You and I have a lot of ground to cover."

"I'm ready when you are."

He gripped his phone tighter. "See you tomorrow evening. Until then, try not to get into trouble."

"What on earth do you mean, *Mr.* Fielding?"

"While you're sightseeing around town, *Ms.* Dorney, don't make the mistake of wandering into The Winds

Saloon. Those poor guys will think Christmas has arrived early. Need I say more?"

He hung up on her sputtering response, aware his grandfather was waiting for him. When he reached the foyer, the older man was leaning on his cane, waiting for him with a worried look on his face. They went into the living room.

"I got a call from Les Nugent a little while ago." Les was a rancher friend of theirs who kept sheep in the same area. "One of his men called him just now. He'd just come down the mountain, but was concerned because he hadn't seen Pali anywhere.

"Apparently some of our sheep were mingling with his. A couple of his men returned them to our herd. They looked around, but there was no sign of Pali. Les wanted me to know." His grandfather looked panicked. "Do you know where he might be?"

Wyatt felt like he'd been kicked in the gut. "I can't imagine, but I'll drive up there at first light. It's possible he went looking for some ewes who wandered off." Except that he had a premonition something much more serious was wrong. His grandfather clearly did, too. The elk hunt was on.

The plan to drive Jenny to Arapahoe would have to be canceled. "I've got to talk to Jenny right now. She's going back to San Francisco tomorrow. I was going to drive her to Jackson, but she'll have to rent a car and get there on her own."

His grandfather put a hand on his arm. "Does that hurt you?"

"Not at all. She's seeing someone and it sounds like it could be serious. I'm happy for her."

Relief broke out on his grandfather's face. "That makes me happy, too."

Wyatt knew why. "I'll tell you all about it later."

He wheeled around and walked back down the hall to the guest bedroom. "Jenny?" He knocked on the door.

"Just a minute." Before long, she opened it wearing a quilted robe. "Hi. What's wrong?"

"My plans have changed." He told her about Pali.

"You go! Don't worry about me. I'll take a taxi to the rental place. They'll have another car waiting for me."

"I'm so sorry, Jenny."

"No, no. If he's in trouble, you've got to find him."

"Thanks for understanding." He kissed her cheek and hurried upstairs to phone Alex.

"Wyatt?" She answered after the first ring.

"Listen to me. An emergency has arisen." He told her the bad news. "I have to go up to the camp first thing in the morning. The problem is, I don't have any idea how long I'll be or what I'll find. I could be gone a day or even a week, depending on the situation.

"Much as I want you to wait until I get back, it wouldn't be fair to you. All I can do is promise to phone you the second I have cell phone service. But if you can't stay long, I understand. I know you've got a job to get back to."

"How soon are you leaving?" she asked.

"Around six in the morning. Right now I've got to hook up the horse trailer and load the truck with provisions and equipment. That'll take me a few hours. If Pali's in some kind of trouble, I've got to reach him quickly."

"Of course! I'm crazy about him. I'll be worried sick until I hear back from you. When you can, promise to call me."

He swallowed hard. "I swear it."

"God bless both of you."

ALEX HUNG UP the phone knowing exactly what she was going to do. Before she'd flown out, she'd bought a new parka, hiking boots, gloves, more rugged jeans and warm tops. After her first experience on the mountain, she planned to be prepared.

She dressed in jeans and a long-sleeved pullover. Once she'd packed her bags, she carried everything down to the lobby and checked out. If the clerk thought it odd that it was three in the morning, he didn't say anything.

A door down the hall led to the hotel parking area. Alex carried her bags to the rental car and took off for Wyatt's ranch. She pulled up in front of the ranch house and just sat there while her heart thumped away. If he left earlier than six, she'd be ready and flash her lights.

At five thirty, she got out and walked around the side with her cases. Sure enough, there he was in the back of the truck putting things away. The light from the back door illuminated his hard-boned features and hunky physique. With the blood pounding in her ears, she approached.

"Hey there, cowboy."

When he looked up and saw her, he almost dropped the bucket he was holding. *"Alex—"*

"It occurred to me you need someone to help you scout for Pali. If he's hurt, I make a pretty good nurse. Fluffy broke me in."

"You shouldn't have come."

At least he hadn't told her to leave. "You and Pali came to my rescue. I'd like to return the favor."

She opened the back door of the truck and put her cases inside. Without waiting for his permission, Alex climbed into the front of the cab and put the article on the dashboard. But she feared that when he got into the truck, he'd tell her to go back to the hotel.

Within minutes the porch light went off and she heard his footsteps come around. He got in behind the wheel. His eyes played over her in the dim light of the interior, filling her with warmth. "That's a new parka." It was midthigh length with a fur-lined hood.

Alex stared at his chiseled profile. "I decided to come to Wyoming prepared this time."

He eyed the papers on the dashboard. "I can't wait to read the article." He started the engine and pulled out to the entrance of the property. A thrill of excitement passed through her to realize they were on their way up the mountain where she'd fallen desperately in love with him.

"The olive color suits you. You look wonderful."

So do you. "I thought the same thing about you

when I saw you in the restaurant wearing a suit." She looked away. "Putting someone on the spot can be a good or bad surprise."

"Frankly, the timing couldn't have been better. I'm glad it happened the way it did."

"Why do you say that?"

"The woman I introduced you to as Rachel Brimley was really Jenny Allen."

Alex inhaled sharply and turned her head to look at him again. "The moment I saw her with you, I thought she must be Jenny."

"You were right. She had her name changed legally a few years back. She doesn't want her parents to find her, so I didn't want to introduce her as Jenny Allen in public, especially in Whitebark."

"Oh, Wyatt—" she cried softly. "After all these years it must have been wonderful to see her." Alex was thrilled for him, but it pained her, too, because Jenny was so lovely and she was sure he couldn't help but love being with her again.

"I consider it a miracle that she's alive and happy."

She moistened her lips nervously. "I'd like to hear all about it, but I'll understand if you'd rather keep it to yourself. How sad you're torn because you're worried about Pali while she's here! Two people you love so much who both need you."

"Jenny's flying back to San Francisco today."

Alex stared into space. "That has to be a really wrenching for you. But at least you know where she is now. When you've found out what's going on with Pali, she'll be there waiting for you."

"Why do you assume that?"

She didn't understand the question. "Because as soon as she was found, she came to Whitebark to be with you."

"It didn't happen like that. Once the attorney gave me her address, I flew to San Francisco and surprised her in her office."

She closed her eyes tightly. "You probably couldn't get there fast enough. I can't even imagine her emotions when she learned you'd been looking for her."

"The reunion was one we'd both needed," he admitted. "But I didn't stay long. She was in the middle of her workday and I had to get back and close down the camp with Pali. That took several days. I also met with a therapist in Riverton."

He'd actually gone? So soon? Alex clenched her hands together, wondering what this all meant. "How did that go?"

"The doctor was very helpful. Talking about everything that has happened cleared up certain murky issues. When I drove home to the ranch yesterday, I discovered Jenny waiting there for me. She and my grandfather were talking up a storm. I knew she'd come because we hadn't had enough time to talk everything out."

So Wyatt hadn't brought her back from San Francisco! The knowledge made Alex's heart beat faster. "Did she have a terrible time in the beginning, all those years ago?"

For the rest of the journey, Alex listened to the whole tragic, amazing story. Jenny Allen was a courageous woman who'd survived against many odds. It was hard not to feel even more sympathetic after learning everything she'd suffered.

"Now that you've been together again, d-do you—"

"Do I know how I feel about her?" he cut in.

She shook her head. "I shouldn't have asked you. Of course you love her. That could never change."

"That's true, but I'm no longer in love with her and haven't been for years."

His answer filled her with joy.

By now the sun had risen above the horizon and they'd driven up over the ridge. In the distance she saw the herd of sheep flocked together. Pali's camper stood alone in the remaining snow. She felt a loss because the tents were no longer present. But the image of the one she'd shared with Wyatt was indelibly impressed on her mind and heart.

Wyatt pulled up close to the camper and turned off the engine. "Come on. Let's go inside and see what we find."

Fear gripped her as they got out. What if they found Pali inside unconscious or ill? Wyatt discovered an unlocked door and climbed in with Alex behind him. She moved to the kitchen while Wyatt walked through, inspecting everything. He came out, turning to her with a bleak expression that broke her heart.

"No sign that he or Gip have been here recently."

She nodded. "Nothing seems to be disturbed. Did he have any weapons?"

"A gun and rifle. They're still on the ledge above the bed. I imagine he went after a ewe last evening and for some reason couldn't make it back. I'm going after him."

"I'll stay here and watch for him while you saddle up your horse. Let me make coffee before you go."

His gaze flicked to hers. "Thanks," he said in a husky voice. "I'm glad you're here."

"I wouldn't be anywhere else."

He caressed her cheek before leaving. She was still quivering from his touch while she got acquainted with the kitchen. Pali was a good housekeeper. Within a few minutes she'd made coffee for them and put sugar in it.

First, she filled a thermos Wyatt could take with him. Then she filled a mug and walked outside. Her heartbreakingly gorgeous rancher had already backed his horse out of the trailer and was ready to go. Besides his rifle, he'd just attached a saddlebag filled most likely with first aid supplies, food and essentials.

She handed him the thermos, which he put inside the bag. Then he reached for the mug. "You're a lifesaver."

Alex wanted to be a lot more than that.

He took several swallows until he'd drained it. She took it from him. "Good luck. I hope you find him fast."

"I have no idea when I'll be back."

"Don't worry about me."

Wyatt's eyes narrowed on her features. "Have you ever handled a gun?"

"Yes. My father took me and my brother target shooting."

"That's good. If Pali should return, fire it in the air to let me know. It's loaded."

She nodded. "Please be careful, Wyatt."

"I'm going to track his footsteps and be back as soon as I can." He gave her a swift kiss on the mouth, then mounted his horse. Before heading farther up the mountain, he rode over to the herd and looked around. She could tell he was trying to figure out where Pali and Gip had gone. Hopefully some evidence was visible to help him.

After a few minutes, he took off up a steep incline. She watched until he disappeared around some large boulders, taking her hopeful, foolish heart with him.

Chapter Eleven

Where are you, old friend?

The higher Wyatt climbed with Rango under a partly cloudy sky, the deeper the snow and the sharper impressions of tracks. Some were made by animals, but others were definitely human.

Please, God, let them be Pali's rather than a hunter's.

Every few steps he called Pali's and Gip's names. At one point he stopped and fired his rifle into the air, then waited to hear a voice.

How far could Pali have gotten on foot? Wyatt was bewildered. He headed toward another set of boulders a little higher up, in the same area where they'd brought down the herd. He shouted their names again and again. But each time, silence followed.

A minute later he rounded the boulders. "Pali? Are you here? Pali?"

Suddenly he heard barking. His heart pounded with excitement. "Gip?"

The sheepdog barked louder. "Keep barking,

boy!" The sound was coming from a small copse of trees.

He guided Rango closer until he found the dog standing over Pali who lay faceup with his eyes closed. There was blood in the snow and all over his left leg. Wyatt leaped from the saddle and hunkered down to examine his friend. He was still alive.

"I'm here, Pali. I'm going to take you home."

Pali's eyelids fluttered open. "Thank God you came. Someone shot me in the leg above the knee right before dark. I couldn't find the bullet. Too much blood. I took off my undershirt and made a tourniquet, but I could only drag myself this far for fear I'd open up the wound again. I had to keep tying and untying the tourniquet all night. The cloth is soaked."

"Don't worry. I'll get you fixed." Wyatt stood up and pulled some things out of the saddlebag, including the thermos. He poured the coffee into the lid, then helped raise Pali's head. "Have some coffee. It'll revive you."

Pali drank it thirstily while Wyatt undid the bloodied rag and applied a fresh tourniquet. "If it weren't for your veterinarian skills, you would have bled to death."

When his friend had finished drinking, Wyatt fed him some painkillers and an antibiotic to start fighting any infection that may have started. Finally, Wyatt put everything back, then helped Pali stand long enough to seat him behind the saddle. The next part was difficult. Thanks to his bull riding training, he managed to swing his own leg over his horse's neck.

"Hold on to me, buddy, and don't fall off. I'll have you down to the camper in no time. Come on, Gip. We're going home."

The dog barked and followed them around the boulders. Pretty soon the band of sheep came into sight. Wyatt headed for the camper. Gip got excited and barked harder.

Pali's camper door flew open. "Gip!" Alex cried. The dog raced toward her and launched himself against her legs. She hugged him like he was an overgrown baby. Wyatt's emotions were on the surface when she raised her blond head. "Oh, Wyatt— you found Pali!"

"He sure did," Pali muttered.

"Thank God you're alive!" She hurried around to help Wyatt steady him. Together they took him inside and laid him on the couch. He had lost a lot of blood and was so weak, his eyelids fluttered.

"He's been shot in the leg. After we've fed him, we'll drive down to the trailhead. From there, we'll be able to phone for Wyoming Life Flight from Casper. They'll transport him to the hospital there."

"Perfect. I have some stew ready, and I've already poured Gip's food and water. While I feed Pali, you load your horse into the trailer. We'll take them down in the truck as soon as you're ready."

Wyatt cupped her face and gave her a fierce kiss. "You're an angel."

Time was of the essence and they worked in harmony. It wasn't long before they helped Pali out to the truck and put him in the front passenger seat in the reclining position. After the camper was locked up, Alex got in the back with Gip.

"What about the sheep?" Pali murmured.

"I'll hire some guys to come up later. Save your strength, buddy."

On the way down, Wyatt met Alex's gaze in the rearview mirror. Her eyes glowed an incandescent green. He couldn't wait to get her alone, but that wouldn't be for some time.

Once he could pick up phone service, he called the hospital in Casper. Arrangements were made for the helicopter to set down at a landing area outside Whitebark.

Wyatt headed for it while Alex brushed the hair off Pali's forehead with tender care. "The helicopter is on the way."

"I don't want to lose my leg."

She kissed Pali's brow. "We won't let that happen."

Wyatt couldn't bear the thought of it. "I'll fly to Casper with him, Alex."

"Of course. I'll drive Gip and me home," she said without blinking an eye. Her courage continued to amaze him. He wondered if she'd ever had to pull a trailer before, but now wasn't the time to ask.

"I'll tell your grandfather to send some men up to watch after the sheep. Leave it to me to take care of everything else until you get back. In case you didn't know, I'm not going anywhere."

If she was sending him a message, he got it loud and clear, and his heart seemed to beat a little faster.

Soon after they reached the landing point, he heard the sound of the rotors and watched the helicopter set down. The next few minutes were critical as the medical team lifted Pali inside, causing Gip to bark his head off.

Alex had gotten out of the truck to watch. Before Wyatt climbed in behind Pali, he gripped her upper arms. "I'll call you the moment I know anything."

She nodded with her heart in her eyes. "He's got to be all right."

Good heaven, how he loved this woman. "Thank you for being here." Wyatt gave her a final kiss and climbed into the helicopter. Already the medical team was going to work on Pali.

"Wyatt?" his friend called to him.

"I'm here, buddy."

ALEX WATCHED THE helicopter rise into the air, taking the man she adored away. *Please don't let anything happen to them.* Her heart was already breaking for Pali, who could lose his leg, but she determined to stay positive. Wyatt would take care of their friend, and everything would be all right.

She climbed into the driver's seat and adjusted it for her legs. "Come on up here, Gip." She patted the front passenger seat so he could be close to her. He leaped forward. "I promise you're going to see Pali again. You're going to have to trust me." She ruffled the fur on his head. "We're headed back to the ranch. I have to tell Wyatt's grandfather what has happened."

The sensation of driving was very different pulling a horse trailer, but this was an emergency. Wyatt was depending on her. She drove slowly, relieved she didn't have to make a lot of turns to reach the ranch.

"So far so good, Gip," she said as she drove in and pulled up to the door at the side of the house. By now, the sun had gone down.

Before doing anything else, she honked. To her relief, Jose came out of the barn. She jumped out of the cab to tell him everything that had happened.

"Don't you worry. I'll take care of Rango and Gip."

But the dog wanted to stay with Alex. "It's okay. I'll just take my bags inside the house and let Mr. Fielding know what's happening."

"He's in the living room eating his dinner in front of the TV." Jose opened the door to the house and helped her inside with her cases. Gip stuck close to her. Otis came running into the kitchen and the two dogs sniffed each other.

"I'll put some food and water out for Gip," Jose offered.

She thanked him while she removed her parka and went over to the sink to wash her hands. Then she walked down the hall to the living room.

Wyatt's grandfather broke into a smile when he saw her come in with both dogs at her side. The TV tray was in front of him. "When did *you* get here?"

"I'll tell you everything in a minute."

"Did you see Wyatt? Is Pali all right?"

Alex patted his arm and sank down on a chair opposite him so he could hear her. "I went up the mountain with Wyatt this morning. Pali got shot. Wyatt has flown to the hospital in Casper with him."

"They have a good trauma center."

"He promised to phone us when he knew anything, Mr. Fielding."

"Call me Royden, remember? What happened?"

"Pali was shot in the leg while looking for a ewe that had wandered off. He lost a lot of blood, but made it through the night by making a tourniquet with strips of his undershirt."

"Pali's the best there is."

"I couldn't agree more. He's worried there's no one up there to look after the sheep."

"After we've heard from Wyatt, I'll call my friend Les and tell him I'll pay his boys to keep watch until I can hire some new shepherds."

"That'll be a relief to Pali. You know, Gip stayed right next to him and kept him warm all night. Talk about devotion. This dog deserves a medal."

"They're man's best friend! Too bad it has to be hunting season. It was one of those damn elk hunters shooting everything in sight and didn't even stop long enough to see if he hit anything!"

"We don't know that for sure."

"Yes, we do. Hell, I shot myself."

Alex burst into laughter. "It's so good to see you again."

He eyed her with pleasure. "What brought you back here?"

Where to start? "I wanted to deliver a copy of my article to Wyatt in person. In fact, it's still out in the truck. I'll get it and show you."

She hurried outside, Gip at her heels. She reached inside to retrieve the sheaf of papers and returned to the house. "Here it is." After handing it to him, she carried the TV tray to the kitchen accompanied by the dog, then returned.

"Hmm. Says here yours will be the lead article? That tells me a lot!"

"My editor liked it, but he's not Wyoming's expert on sheep. While we wait for a call from Wyatt, go ahead and read it. I hope I'm brave enough to hear your review when you've finished."

He laughed and plunged in.

Too many emotions were attacking Alex for her to sit still. She got up and took her bags to the guest bedroom to stay busy. On her way back to the living room, she stopped in the kitchen and poured herself a cup of coffee that was still warm in the pot.

Holding her breath, she crept into the living room, almost afraid to hear what he had to say.

Royden lifted his head. "Does he have any idea that quote you started out with would end up in print?"

"Oh—you mean the one that says, 'If the lamb lovers of this world knew what we go through, they'd pay us billions for the privilege of being served lamb chops and roasts at the dinner table'?"

He nodded.

"Yes. I asked if I could quote him and he gave me his permission."

Laughter poured out of Royden.

She eyed him. "I'm waiting."

He sat forward. "That blizzard brought more information out of him than I would have imagined. Like I told you before, your editor knew what he was doing when he hired you. You're brilliant at your job."

"Thank you."

"That article means Wyatt has actually listened to me all these years. Who would have thought?"

Now Alex was laughing. "You mean you believed everything had fallen on deaf ears?"

"It was hard to tell with that unhappy grandson of mine. The poor kid was terrified of the mountains."

Her laughter faded. "I know. He told me."

"Now he ambles around the boulders like the sheep and fights fires."

"You should have seen him mount Rango today and attack the mountain looking for Pali." Her voice caught. "The man is fearless."

Royden stared at her. "He's changed since you flew out to Wyoming the first time. Tell me why you really came back. Don't you think it's time?"

Her cell rang before she could answer him. She pulled the phone out of her pocket. The second she saw the caller ID she clicked on. "Wyatt?"

"Good news. Pali's not going to lose his leg. It was

a flesh wound. The reason he couldn't find the bullet was because there was an exit wound he couldn't feel."

"Oh, thank heaven. Listen, Wyatt. I'm going to put my phone on speaker and hold it up to your grandfather. We're both in the living room talking. Tell him what you told me. It'll relieve him. Just a minute."

She got up and stood right in front of Royden. "It's Wyatt. He's going to talk to both of us." Alex put the phone near him.

"Wyatt?" his grandfather called out.

"Hi, Grandad. I've got the best news in the world for you." Alex stayed right there and held the phone while the two men had a long conversation. "I've phoned his family. His father has a passport and will take the next flight to the US. I'll stay with him until he arrives.

"The doctor says there wasn't as much loss of blood as first suspected. He's been put on antibiotics and will be fit to travel in a few days with crutches. I've told him that he and his father can stay with us while he recovers."

"Good. I wouldn't have him stay anywhere else."

"Alex?" Wyatt said her name in a way that let her know this was for her alone.

She moved to the chair so they could talk privately for a moment and took off the speaker. "Yes?"

"Don't you dare go anywhere. Do you hear me?"

At this point she was trembling from happiness.

"I won't. When you fly back, I'll drive to Jackson Hole to pick you up."

"I'm counting the minutes. Before I hang up, Pali wants a progress report on Gip."

With tear-filled eyes she looked down at the dog. "He's right here at my feet."

"In case you weren't already aware, Pali's as crazy about you as his dog."

"Give him my love and take care of yourself, Wyatt."

"Alex?"

"Yes?"

"There's someone else who's crazy about you, and I'm not talking about my grandfather."

Wyatt... "You must mean my father and brother," she teased to cover her emotions.

"Guess again. Talk to you soon. It won't be long now. Once we're together I promise there won't be any more interruptions." He clicked off.

She loved him so much she could hardly breathe. After hanging up, she put the phone back in her pocket.

Royden fixed his gaze on her. "I'm still waiting for an answer to my question."

"I would tell you, but don't you think your grandson should hear it first?"

His eyes glistened. "I wish my wife were still alive so she'd see my experiment worked. Wyatt is in love with the blond-haired angel who's the most beautiful sight ever to walk inside this house."

Alex smiled. "That was very clever of you to send me up the mountain with the storm coming on."

"I could tell by the way you were looking at Wyatt's picture that you wouldn't mind too much."

"Your ploy worked. *In spades.*"

"That's all I wanted to hear."

Chapter Twelve

Wyatt took a strong liking to Pali's father, Domeka Vizkaya, the moment he came into the hospital in Casper. They talked for several hours, both with Pali and apart from him.

The doctor indicated Pali could be released late the next day. He wanted to be sure there was no infection and that Pali could manage his crutches. Until then, Domeka could stay in Pali's room. Wyatt had already paid for their flights to Jackson Hole and would pick them up.

Pali told Wyatt to get out of there and go home. That was music to his ears. Instead of calling Alex, he took the next flight to Jackson Hole and drove a rental car to the ranch. Her rental wasn't there.

His brow furrowed as he raced through the house to find her. Relieved to see her belongings in the guest bedroom, he walked to the living room. His grandfather happened to be napping in his favorite chair with Otis at his feet. She had to be outside, maybe taking a walk.

He hurried out the back door. On a hunch, he

walked toward the barn. As Wyatt headed toward Fluffy's stall, Gip rushed over to him, barking happily and brushing against his legs.

Wyatt patted the dog's head and moved past him to see Alex filling the ewe's feed bowl.

"I might have known I'd find you in here. I think I've got competition."

She wheeled around. "Wyatt!" The light in her eyes told him everything he needed to know. She put the sack down. "I've been waiting for a phone call," she said breathlessly.

"I wanted to surprise you. Come in the house with me."

She followed him out of the barn. Fluffy wasn't happy and let out several cries. They walked through the house to the staircase and went upstairs.

"Sorry, Gip. You'll have to wait outside." He shut his bedroom door on the dog, ignoring the barking. The sight of this beautiful woman in his bedroom consumed him to the exclusion of all else.

They stood close to each other. His eyes had fastened on her. "I only have one question for you."

"The answer is yes," she answered boldly before he could ask it. "I love you so terribly, I've been in pain ever since our first night in the tent and flew here to tell you.

"The truth is, I never wanted to leave you. When you received the news about Jenny, I felt you needed your space, so I left. But I almost died waiting to learn what you'd decided to do. I couldn't help wondering, if you saw her again, would it rekindle old feelings? If you didn't, would you carry that terrible pain around forever?

"My fear of being clingy stopped me from reaching out to you, so I used the finished article as an excuse to see you again. Then when I saw you with Jenny I couldn't imagine you not wanting her. Wyatt—if you don't love me like I love you—"

He cupped her gorgeous face in his hands. "If I hadn't been afraid of offending you and breaking every rule in the book, I would have turned those days and nights during the storm into our honeymoon. I've been in love with you from the moment you climbed down from Jose's truck. You *know* that.

"I wanted to tell you what you meant to me while we spent the night in the forest, but I knew I had to take care of a few matters first, to put away the past once and for all." He took a deep breath. "Before I kiss you, I'm going downstairs to let Grandad know I'm home. I'll only be gone a minute, then I'll be back up. Don't you dare leave this room."

The love lighting her beautiful green eyes transformed him. "I'm staying right here."

Wyatt spun around and left the room. "Come on, Gip." The dog reluctantly followed him down the stairs.

By now, his grandfather was awake. He looked up at Wyatt. "I heard you come in a while ago, but you were in such a hurry I didn't want to detain you. What are you doing down here?"

A smile broke out on Wyatt's face. He might have

known there were no secrets in this house. "I wanted to let you know I was back."

The older man laughed. He pulled some papers from the side of his chair. "Here. One of these days when you don't have anything else in the world to do, you'll want to read Alex's article. I have something else for you, too." He reached into his shirt pocket. Wyatt couldn't imagine what his grandfather was up to.

"I gave this to your grandmother. I'd sure like to see it remain in the family."

Wyatt stared at the gold wedding ring with the small solitaire diamond. It glinted up at him. *"Grandad—"*

"Jenny told me everything before she left for the airport. I know for a fact she was excited to fly back to San Francisco."

Love for his grandfather welled up in Wyatt's chest. He leaned over and hugged him.

"Now, if you really want to make me happy, get out of here!"

Wyatt dashed from the living room. In the background he heard his grandfather order Gip to stay put.

Taking the stairs two at a time, he headed for his bedroom and opened the door. He put the article on the nearest chair.

Alex had been standing at one of the windows, looking out at the mountains. The light illuminated the silvery strands in her blond hair. She turned when she heard him enter. He could hardly believe this beautiful, warm, wonderful woman loved him the way he loved her.

In the next breath she ran to him. He pulled her into his arms and swung her around. "Alex," he groaned before following her body down to the bed. Wyatt thrust his hands into her hair and began kissing her.

The sun was at a different angle in the sky when he finally relinquished her lips so she could breathe. "I can't get enough of you."

"I feel the same way about you. I'm afraid I love you too much."

"Does that mean you'll marry me as soon as we can make it happen?"

"Yes! Oh, yes!" She covered his face with kisses.

"That's what I needed to hear." He rolled away enough to pull the wedding ring out of his shirt pocket. Reaching for her left hand, he slid it on her ring finger. "This was my grandmother's."

She held up her hand and gasped.

"When I went downstairs, Grandad said he wanted me to keep it in the family and handed it to me. That should tell you exactly how he feels about you. Will you accept it as an engagement ring?"

"Wearing her ring means everything to me. I love it! She knew what you needed to be whole again and encouraged you to get help. If you hadn't heeded her wisdom, you and I might not be together now."

"You're right." He gave her another passionate kiss. "As for me, I have my own ideas about the wedding ring I want to give you."

Her eyes shone like stars. "I love your grandfather for this. I love you. Oh, Wyatt—I've never been so happy in my life." She launched herself at him so he fell back. Once again they lost track of time and their surroundings while they expressed their pent-up desire.

Sometime later he looked up at her. "Will you marry me right away?"

"Right now, if we could."

"That's good because I'd like to keep this a white wedding."

She groaned. "Then we should set the earliest date possible."

"Agreed. I'm already out of control holding you in my arms. What about your job?"

Alex told him the situation with her boss. "I'm going to turn down the promotion, but I'm pretty sure he'll allow me to continue covering stories. The difference will be that I'll write them from here."

"When you travel, I'll arrange to go with you when I can. We'll turn your first assignment into our honeymoon. What do you think?"

She sighed. "I think I'm dreaming."

"What about your apartment?"

"The yearly lease is up next month. No problem there."

Overjoyed, he rolled her onto her back. "Where do you want to be married?"

"Right here in Whitebark, at church in front of your grandfather and friends."

"What about your parents?"

"They helped put on a huge wedding in New Jersey for my brother and his fiancée. But I know for a fact they'll want to see me married here. They're very much aware that this place is already home to me. I got my life back when I flew out here the first time."

Adrenaline flooded Wyatt's system. "We'll have the reception here at the house and hire a catering service. Martha will help. So will Jose and Maria."

"That's perfect. I'll ask my family to fly out a few days ahead of time. They'll bring my belongings with them. My niece, Katy, will make an adorable flower girl. They'll all love getting to know your grandfather and will do what they can. They'll love you!"

She kissed him again until they were both breathless, but Wyatt was reaching flash point. With reluctance, he moved away from her and got to his feet. "Let's phone your parents now and set the date with them."

She moved off the bed and put her arms around his neck. "What about Pali?"

"I don't know. He has a new girlfriend at home. Something tells me he's going to want to get back to her as soon as he can. Much as I'd like him to come to our wedding, I don't think it's going to happen."

"That's understandable." She smiled in that enticing way. "Are you going to ask your firefighter friends to stand up for you?"

"Since my brother isn't here to do it, I was thinking of them."

"Will you wear your firefighter dress uniform for the ceremony?"

A chuckle escaped. "Would it mean that much to you?"

"Yes. I fell in love with your photograph first. When your grandfather said you were a sheep rancher, too, I was in complete awe. And when he offered to get Jose to drive me up to the camp so I could interview you, I went right along with it, never once thinking of saying no." She kissed his mouth. "Your charisma is too overpowering."

He rubbed his hands up and down her arms. "It will take all day and night to explain what you do to me, but first we'd better make that phone call."

"Let's do it downstairs after we tell your grand-father."

Her words caused his throat to swell. "Thank you for loving him."

"I couldn't help it. Did I tell you what he said when I first arrived at the house for the interview?"

"Enlighten me."

"He didn't like it that I had a man's name. Then he said, and I quote, 'With that blond hair and the face of an angel, you're the most beautiful sight ever to walk inside this house.'"

Evidently it had been love at first sight for his grandfather, too.

"No doubt he swept your grandmother off her feet with words like that. I can understand why they had such a great marriage. What woman could be immune to such flattery?"

Wyatt's gaze took in every delectable feature. "He got that right about you and knew I'd collapse on the spot when you showed up at the camp." Filled with insatiable desire, he devoured her one more time before they left his bedroom to plan their future.

THE SUITES AT the Whitebark Hotel, where Alex's parents and family were staying, had been turned into a bridal bower. Katy, looking adorable in a white lace dress, ran from one room to another doing errands while all three women got ready to leave for the church in their wedding finery.

Both Alex's mother and Natalie wore soft peach gowns. Alex had finished putting on her makeup. She stood in front of the mirror in her parents' room for one final inspection.

When her family had flown out three days ago, they'd gone shopping for her wedding dress while they were still in Jackson Hole. She'd found a fabulous white, long-sleeved bohemian-style sheath in lace and chiffon. It had a bateau neckline and godets in the floor-length skirt. Over her hair she wore a chapel-length lace veil. She wanted Wyatt to "almost" collapse when he saw her.

Flush-faced and way too excited to stand still any longer, Alex finally left the hotel with the others. The cool October afternoon air felt good against her hot cheeks. Katy carried the bouquet for her.

Jeff and her father were waiting out in front for them in a rental van. They planned to drive to the Fieldings' family church a mile away for the four-o'clock ceremony.

"You're glowing," her dad said as he helped her inside. "That's what real happiness does to you."

"It's Wyatt's fault."

"I know." Her father kissed her cheek. "You're both lucky to have found each other."

WYATT DROVE HIS grandfather to the church in his car; Jose and his wife followed in theirs. Together they helped Royden inside.

The older man wore his old dress blues from a former time, looking very distinguished. After much pleading from Alex, Wyatt wore his Class A blue dress firefighter uniform with the gold buttons. He explained to her that the three gold stripes on the sleeves represented nine years of service. Under his arm he carried his blue-and-gold dress hat.

Organ music, along with fragrance from the flowers, filled the church that was overflowing with guests. Soon the minister appeared, followed by Porter and Cole in their dress blues. Holden wore his sheriff's dress uniform in dark brown with gold braid on the sleeves. They came to stand next to Wyatt.

Cole flashed Wyatt a meaningful glance. "It'll be over before you know it," he whispered. "Hang in there." If anyone understood how eager Wyatt felt to be with his bride, Cole did. He'd been forced to wait nine years to marry the love his life.

Wyatt's gaze flicked to the church pews packed with friends. Besides Jose and Martha and their families, Alex's family sat up front by his grandfather, warming his heart. He liked her family very much.

While he was taking it all in, the organist started to play the wedding march.

His heart beat wildly as Katy started up the aisle from the rear of the chapel. Then came Alex, holding on to the arm of her father. He led her to Wyatt's side. Those green eyes lifted to him. She was so breathtaking, he couldn't think.

"Dearly beloved," the minister began.

The rest was like a dream. He recalled saying *I do* and hearing Alex's identical response. Rings were exchanged. He'd bought an emerald solitaire set in gold that looked beautiful next to his grandmother's ring. To his shock, Alex had given him a man's stunning gold band with a horizontal strip of four sapphires.

"I now pronounce you, Wyatt, and you, Alex, husband and wife. May your joy be full. You may now kiss your bride."

At last.

He lowered his mouth to hers, but kept it light. If she wondered why, he'd let her know later that he feared he'd lose control and forget they had an audience.

Gripping her hand, he walked her down the aisle. They stepped outside the church to the blare of a siren. The other guys had driven the fire truck down to the church. There must have been a dozen of them in dress uniform, including the captain, Chief Powell and the fire commissioner, lined up beside it to salute them.

"Oh, Wyatt—" Alex grabbed his arm. "They all love you so much!"

"You're wrong. They came to see what *you* look like. The stories have been spreading about the knockout woman from New York who got stranded on the mountain with me during the storm. I'll never live it down. And you know something? I don't mind, because those were the most magical days and nights of my life. In fact, I'm so hungry for you, I'm going to kiss you again, but this time I might never stop."

"Then we'd better not touch each other yet," she said. "We have a reception to get through first."

"Just one kiss, sweetheart, to keep your husband going. Remember, you promised to obey me."

"No, I didn't. I promised to love and cherish you."

"It's the same thing," he murmured against her lips, giving her no chance to argue. The second he did what he was dying to do, the guys clapped and whistled in delight. Life didn't get better than this.

BY TEN O'CLOCK that night, the house had emptied. The caterers were gone. Alex's family had gone back to the hotel. They'd be flying to New York tomorrow.

Royden had gone to bed. Gip had become their temporary house pet until Pali returned. He and Otis were starting to tolerate each other. Wyatt was locking up before coming up to the bedroom.

Their bedroom now.

Alex had taken a shower, relishing the signs of Wyatt's occupation. A man's bathroom, but it wouldn't be for long.

Her heart thudded painfully while she waited for her husband. She'd put on a new nightgown and peignoir in a cream color with lace. He'd looked so spectacular in his uniform, she hadn't been able to take her eyes off him all night. The ache for him had reached its zenith.

After turning down the bed, she put a gift on his pillow and sat next to it. Secretly, she'd asked Royden to get out some old pictures of Wyatt's family—he didn't have many. And she'd pored through them. One colored photo had caught at her heart.

It showed him and his older brother in the family pumpkin patch, sitting on some huge pumpkins. Their mom and dad were behind them. All of them were laughing.

The adorable picture was so precious, she'd gone into town and had it enlarged to an eight by ten. After finding the perfect frame, she'd gift wrapped it to give it to him on their wedding night.

She was so deep in thought, she didn't realize he'd come into the room.

"Sweetheart?" Wyatt said in a husky voice.

She got up from the bed. He'd taken off his uniform jacket and rolled up the sleeves of his white shirt. She'd never seen a more spectacular man in her life. And now he was her husband forever.

"I thought you'd never get here."

His blue eyes blazed with desire as they traveled over every inch of her. Then he saw the package. "What have you got there?"

"A small gift for you."

He came closer. "Can I have it now?"

Over the short time she'd known him, Alex had come to realize he was like any little boy who couldn't wait for his treats. She handed it to him. On the top she'd put one word on the little white card. *Beloved.*

She heard his quick intake of breath before he took off the wrapping paper. It was probably five minutes before he lifted his head. Alex had never seen tears in his eyes, but they were filled with them now.

"There's nothing in this world you could have given me that would mean more to me," he whispered. "I love you, Alex."

"I love *you* and I want us to have our own family and grow pumpkins and ride horses together and camp out in the mountains by the sheep. You're going to be the most fabulous father."

"And you're going to be an amazing mother. I knew it when I saw you inside the tent next to Fluffy. Seeing how kind and thoughtful you were to a lonely, helpless creature did it for me. I knew I had to have you."

"You've got me now, my love."

"Give me a few minutes to shower, then I'm all yours."

She smiled. "That's what you said to me that afternoon in the tent. When you lay down on that blanket, I wanted to crawl over and snuggle in your arms."

"I was willing you to come."

"You know why I didn't."

His eyes darkened with emotion. "Promise me you'll never hold back again."

"I promise. Now please hurry and take that shower."

He set the picture on the dresser and disappeared into the bathroom. While he was gone she turned off the light. After removing her peignoir she got into bed and lay on her side. Before long he emerged from the bathroom with a towel hitched around his hips.

She felt the mattress dip and suddenly she was pulled into his arms. Their legs entwined. He buried his face in her hair.

"Alex—" His voice was low and rough. "I need you more than life itself. Love me, darling. Never stop."

Her heart was too full to answer. All she could do was show him. But he was the one to show her a wedding night that was glorious beyond comprehension. The loving, the giving, the exquisite joy of worshipping each other with their bodies transcended everything she'd ever thought about lovers.

Throughout the night they found new ways to please each other. She was thankful they'd waited until now. No shadow marred their happiness. When she awakened the next day, he was still asleep. Alex should have been exhausted, too, but she'd never been more wide-awake.

She lay against his strong shoulder and studied the beauty of his face for another hour. He was a quiet sleeper. His black hair curled near his neck. She played with it while she waited for him to feel her against him and reach for her. This was going to be her life for as long as they lived.

Sheer ecstasy.

No woman had ever been this blessed, especially when he woke up all of a sudden and started making love to her again with almost fierce passion. Later, after they were both sated, he let out a strange sound.

"What's the matter?" she asked, pressing closer against him.

His eyes searched hers with an intensity that surprised her. "Before I woke up earlier, I was dreaming that I'd lost you. I was so terrified, I fought my way out of it. That's when I felt you next to me."

"I've been right here. I'll always be right here." But she realized her husband was still haunted by past losses. Too many. She wondered if dreams like that would plague him for the rest of his life, but she refused to worry about that now.

Epilogue

Nine months later

AFTER HER LATEST morning checkup, Alex left her OB's office at the Whitebark hospital excited by what he'd told her, but almost afraid to tell Wyatt. He'd come with her to most of her appointments, but he'd been called into a meeting at the fire station with the big brass and wouldn't be home until later. He hadn't wanted to leave her, but she'd told him he *had* to go.

On her way back to the ranch, she stopped in to see Cole's wife, Tamsin, at the CPA firm where she worked. Since the wedding they'd become good friends. Tamsin and her sister, Sally, were fun to be with—both had babies and were thrilled that Alex had gotten pregnant so fast.

They often went to lunch together with Heather, a girl from Tamsin's firm. Over the last nine months or so, they'd gone to parties together with their husbands. Alex enjoyed the camaraderie and was starting to feel a true connection with Wyatt's world. It was so great to have close friends, and today Alex needed input from someone she trusted.

She parked the car and went inside, walking past the reception area to Tamsin's office. Her friend looked up at her with a smile. "I think you need to sit down. You look ready to deliver. Do I ever remember how that felt."

Alex nodded. "That's why I'm here. My due date isn't for a week, but the doctor says the baby has dropped. It'll probably come in the next twelve to twenty-four hours. My folks are ready to fly out at any time."

Tamsin frowned. "Why aren't you happier about it?"

"If I tell you something, you have to promise you'll never repeat it to anyone, especially not Cole. If Wyatt found out I'd told your husband anything about him, it would hurt him. I probably shouldn't be saying anything to you, but I need someone to confide in."

"You have my word, Alex. And this is a good time for me to talk. I don't have a client until this afternoon."

Alex took a fortifying breath. "You and I have shared a lot of private things about our husbands. For different reasons, neither of their roads was easy. But there's one thing I've kept to myself. It's about Wyatt's nightmares."

Her friend broke into a frown. "That doesn't sound good."

"They always have to do with him losing me. And he phones me a lot during the day."

"After what you've told me of his past, it's understandable."

"I agree, but when I tell him the baby could come anytime now, I—I guess I'm afraid it could make them worse," she stammered.

Tamsin eyed her with compassion. "This has to do with losing Jenny and the baby, of course."

"Before we were married, he consulted a psychiatrist in Riverton. Wyatt told me it helped him with some murky issues, so I believed he'd gotten past them. But I'm afraid it isn't true. For the last two months his anxiety has grown worse. I tell him to go and do his work, but he never wants to leave. It's been driving me crazy. He wants to wait on me and fights me when I tell him not to fuss. He broods and walks around with a pained expression, like he's afraid to leave the house. When he's gone, he phones almost on the hour unless he's in a meeting like today. Frankly, I could use any advice you've got for me."

"Well…if I were you, this is what I would do."

Alex listened to her friend. Her advice was so simple, Alex was shocked and ashamed that she hadn't thought of it herself.

After thanking Tamsin profusely, she left her friend and hurried back to the ranch. Royden was ready for his lunch. Alex fixed them soup and sandwiches. He liked eating lunch on the TV tray in the living room so he could watch his favorite shows.

Since the wedding, they'd had no more need of Martha. Alex had taken over the cooking. She'd liked to cook growing up, and since moving in with Wyatt she'd learned lots more, some from watching Martha. Wyatt did the housecleaning with her. She loved this life and adored his grandfather who was a pleasure to live with. He was excited about the advent of a great-grandson.

Once they'd eaten she served Royden some ice cream. He darted her a glance. "Have you decided what you're going to name the baby?"

"To be honest, we had names for a girl or a boy picked out before we knew we were expecting a boy. It'll be Ryan Dorney Fielding after Wyatt's brother. He's going to be arriving very soon." They'd already made a nursery upstairs in the smaller room across the hall from their bedroom.

Royden smiled. "If I don't miss my guess, Ida picked him out to send to you."

"That wouldn't surprise me. I'm so sorry I never got to meet her."

"One day you will."

Alex nodded and picked up their empty lunch trays to return them to the kitchen. After telling him she was going upstairs to their bedroom to rest, her first act was to phone the fire station on the business line. She asked for Wyatt to call her, but he was to be told that it was *not* an emergency. Within five minutes her phone rang. She picked up.

"Alex?" He sounded almost frantic.

"Hi, darling. How's it going?"

"What's wrong?" he blurted in a panicked voice, ignoring her question.

"Not a thing. The doctor says I'm in wonderful shape. If I have a problem, it's because I'm missing you."

"I haven't been able to think about anything but you," he answered after a long pause, with a world of emotion in his voice. Tamsin was a genius.

"All we've done is talk about the baby, but I'm lonely for my husband."

"Alex—"

"I wish you'd tell Chief Powell that I need you now. I want you to come home so we can concentrate on each other until after the baby is born." It did sound divine. "You and I need some private time. Tell Jose and Pali you're taking care of me. It's time you and I forgot the world."

Again a silence. Then, "Sweetheart?"

Whatever she'd said was working. Alex could tell it by the way she'd caught her wonderful husband so off guard. His voice trembled.

"What is it?"

"Nothing."

"How about bringing Chinese for your grandfather? He loves it."

"I'll be right there." And he hung up.

She loved him.

Alex took another shower and put on a new nightgown in a sea-green color with lace. She put on earrings to match. Last week, she and the girls had gone shopping for her and the baby.

After a glance in the mirror she noticed that her hair had grown longer and curlier. He'd said more than once he liked it this way. After applying fresh makeup and lipstick, she felt as ready as she could be, considering she was big with child.

Before she lounged on her side on the bed, she opened the windows to let in the warm breeze. Summer had come. Their baby was almost here. It was time to let Wyatt know he was her whole world. That was all the reassurance he needed.

Within a half hour she heard footsteps racing up the stairs. He must have broken every record to get here this fast. As he opened the door, she smiled up at her cherished husband who owned her heart and soul. "I thought you'd never get here," she teased.

Wyatt stood stock-still for a minute while he appraised every line and curve of her.

"I love you. Come closer and just hold me."

Their eyes fused. His blazed a scorching blue. In the next instant he joined her on the bed and gave her a kiss to die for.

"This is heaven," she murmured sometime later.

He burrowed his face in her neck. "You're my whole life. You know that, don't you?"

"We're so blessed to have found each other." Tears of love burned her eyes. "Do you know, when I flew out here the first time, I remember sitting in the taxi thinking that life was flat and the fulfillment I craved probably wasn't possible.

"When your grandfather urged me to go up to the sheep camp to talk to you, I took another look at the picture of you on the mantel in your dress blues and knew I had to go, no matter what. Something deep inside told me I was in for an experience I didn't dare miss."

He gave her a long, passionate kiss. "After you and I were married, he admitted that he'd known about the approaching storm and argued with Jose, who didn't think it wise to take you up there. But his will prevailed, thank God."

"I noticed how fast Jose took off after I climbed out of the truck. If I hadn't been in shock meeting you in the flesh, a man more gorgeous than his photograph, I would have realized something odd was going on. We have your grandfather to thank for our happiness."

She threw her arm around his neck. "Thank you for coming home so quickly. I need you like I've never needed you before."

As her doctor had predicted, her water broke nine hours later and then came the pains. Wyatt was right there and drove her to the hospital where her OB eventually told her she'd broken every record in the book by having such a short labor.

Once their perfect baby, Ryan, was delivered, the doctor smiled at her. "What's your secret? Every woman should be so lucky."

Alex eyed her handsome husband while he inspected every part of their adorable son. One day soon she'd thank Tamsin for her inspired solution that had ended the painful cycle of anxiety for Wyatt.

When he looked up at her with tears in his eyes, she saw no shadows, only a fullness of joy. Ah...this was just the beginning.

* * * * *

We hope you enjoyed this story from
Harlequin® Western Romance.

Harlequin® Western Romance is coming to an
end, but community, cowboys and true love are
here to stay. Starting July 2018, discover more
heartfelt tales of family and friendship from
Harlequin® Special Edition.

Romance is for life, and these stories show that
every chapter in a relationship has its challenges
and delights and that love can be
renewed with each turn of the page!

Look for six *new* romances every month
from **Harlequin® Special Edition!**
Available wherever books are sold.

SPECIAL EXCERPT FROM

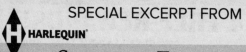

HARLEQUIN

SPECIAL EDITION

*Days before her thirtieth birthday, Allegra Clark finds
herself a runaway bride and accidentally crashing a
birthday party for Zander Wilde—the man who promised
to marry her if neither of them was married by thirty…*

Read on for a sneak preview of
HOW TO ROMANCE A RUNAWAY BRIDE,
*the next book in the **WILDE HEARTS** miniseries,*
by Teri Wilson.

Is that what you want? The question was still there, in his
eyes. All she had to do was decide.

She took a deep breath and shook her head.

Zander leaned closer, his eyes hard on hers. Then he
reached to cup her face with his free hand and drew the
pad of his thumb slowly, deliberately along the swell of
her bottom lip. "Tell me what you want, Allegra."

You. She swallowed. *I want you.*

"This," she said, reaching up on tiptoe to close the
space between them and touch her lips to his.

What are you doing? Stop.

But it was too late to change her mind. Too late to
pretend she didn't want this. Because the moment her
mouth grazed Zander's, he took ownership of the kiss.

His hands slid into her hair, holding her in place, while
his tongue slid brazenly along the seam of her lips until
they parted, opening for him.

Then there was nothing but heat and want and the
shocking reality that this was what she'd wanted all
along. Zander.

Had she always felt this way? It seemed impossible. Yet beneath the newness of his mouth on hers and the crush of her breasts against the solid wall of his chest, there was something else. A feeling she couldn't quite put her finger on. A sense of belonging. Of destiny.

Home.

Allegra squeezed her eyes closed. She didn't want to imagine herself fitting into this life again. There was too much at stake. Too much to lose. But no matter how hard she railed against it, there it was, shimmering before like her a mirage.

She whimpered into Zander's mouth, and he groaned in return, gently guiding her backward until her spine was pressed against the cool marble wall. Before she could register what was happening, he gathered her wrists and pinned them above her head with a single, capable hand. And the last remaining traces of resistance melted away. She couldn't fight it anymore. Not from this position of delicious surrender. Her arms went lax, and somewhere in the back of her mind, a wall came tumbling down.

The breath rushed from her body, and a memory came into focus with perfect, crystalline clarity.

Let's make a deal. If neither of us is married by the time we turn thirty, we'll marry each other. Agreed?

Agreed?

Don't miss
HOW TO ROMANCE A RUNAWAY BRIDE
by Teri Wilson, available July 2018 wherever
Harlequin® Special Edition books and ebooks are sold.

www.Harlequin.com

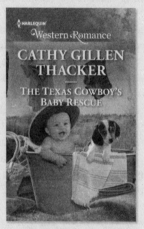